ADAM

CLAIRE STOLWORTHY

ADAM

All rights reserved © 2021 C.M. Stolworthy

The right of C.M. Stolworthy to be identified as author of this work has been asserted in accordance with section 77 of the Copyright, Designs and Patents Act 1988

CHAPTER 1

*B*ees... who would've thought? Well, those scientists did. A population out of control. Not enough food to feed them and Bee's the answer. Except they weren't the answer those scientists couldn't have got it more wrong if they had tried. The contraceptive drug they came up with wiped out almost half the populations of the world.

Why was I thinking this? Mainly because my demise was imminent, and that alone was causing my mind to come up with a solution. An escape plan, my survival instinct kicking into action. How ironic as I was the solution. My attention drifted back to the winter scene beyond the window. Anything to distract myself from my immediate future.

Watching the snow, I can see my reflection in the glass. Pale hair teasing blue eyes too big for my face. They follow the drifting flake as it touches the moisture and dissolves. As death will dissolve me in a hand full of years. Nothing to mark my existence or passing. A shudder rattles my frame as I push away the melancholy thoughts. Unless…

'Concentrate Adam,' her stick raps against my easel and I startle.

'Yes, Madam Montreal,' willing away the blush that climbs my face.

Glancing out of the window, my fingers guide the pencil across the paper. Scrunching my face in concentration. I block out the sounds of the boys playing in the snow as I try to capture the energy and enthusiasm of their robust game.

'Ah Adam, yes, firmer strokes with the pencil,' My art teacher guides my hand over the paper. 'Yes, much better,' she praises as she moves away, her familiar scent distracting me. 'I will expect you in my class tomorrow with this finished,' she smiles at me before leaving by a side door. Her shoes echoing on the wooden floor. I concentrate in silence. Just the sound of my pencil on the paper.

'Adam, where are you?' A gust of freezing air follows the voice as Mathew bursts into the room. He shuffles over to the fire and sits as close as he can without setting himself on fire. For a moment I picture this in my head ending with him running about in a flame like coat setting the entire school burning. Blinking, I focus on him again.

'Ah, you have finished your art lesson,' Mathews features light up with mischief and I inwardly groan as I try to work out what it is he is plotting.

'Why? What's going on?' His damp, dishevelled state brings a smile to my face. With Auburn hair plastered to his forehead and his face pinker than normal. This suggests that he was involved in the snowball fight, possibly the instigator. He watches me drawing for a bit before answering.

'Oh, they're organising a snowball fight between the Mothers and the boys, if you're interested.' His gaze travels to my face as his mouth turns up in a smile, his green eyes shining.

'Oh, I see. Do you mind if I pass?' Sucking my pencil, I study my drawing. 'I have to finish this for tomorrow.'

He peers over my shoulder. 'You know you are very good'

he leans back. 'You make me look so handsome,' He turns his head striking a pose. With a laugh, I push him away from my drawing.

'Get out,' my voice teasing. He wanders over to the door, puts his hand on the handle, and turns to me.

'Catch you later,' pulling it closed behind him. My solitude is short-lived, however, as I soon hear the voice of my Mother. A resigned sigh passes my lips at the thought of this next interruption.

'Adam, Adam, sample time,' she says in a singsong voice. She opens the door and steps inside, smiling at me, waggling a sample pot in her fingers. Her impossibly high heels clacking on the wooden floor, long blonde hair loose down her back.

'Why weren't you outside?' She asks, sitting on the sofa to my side. Well, sitting isn't quite right, perching would be more accurate. She crosses her long slender legs.

Taking in her form-fitting dress and low neckline that doesn't leave much to the imagination, I shrug, meeting her gaze. 'Had an art lesson.'

'Yes, of course you did. It's very warm in here, are you ill?' She reaches out and strokes my face with her fingers, before ruffling my hair. She does this on purpose, as she knows I hate her messing with my hair.

'No, I'm fine,' a frown forming with annoyance as I growl at her and push her hand away. Her lips twitch as she suppresses a smile.

'Good, right, well, sample time? Are you ready or do you want some help?' She runs her hand up my inner thigh, stroking and caressing.

'No, I don't need any help.' Her hand rests on my crotch, closing my eyes, relaxing my body. 'Do we have to do this can't we just skip it today? I'm not feeling too into it.' Casting my eyes upward, I wait for her reaction.

'You weren't feeling very into it last time either, or were you unwell? It's difficult to keep track. Come on, what's gotten into you?'

'It's just, what's the rush? If there are only so many samples that can be taken, why the big hurry to get them all out of the way now? Why can't we... you know, space them out a bit, take it easy?'

'Adam, not collecting your sample will not stop you from being retired at twenty. That's just the way it works, honey. All that will happen is that I will get into trouble for not meeting my quota. I can't keep making excuses for you.' Worry in her voice as her eyes sweep over my body.

'But I don't want to be retired at twenty. I want to have a nice, long, happy life. And what with the downturn, hardly anyone can afford to buy an Adam nowadays. What if nobody wants me and I don't sell?' I complained. Not that I want that either. I want to be my own person, not some woman's property.

Somewhere in the world, there must be a place for me. A place where I can live in peace. I want to fall hopelessly in love. Like the characters in the books, I enjoy reading. I want to try strange and exotic food, step into the ocean and feel sand between my toes as waves crash against the shore. A defeated sigh escapes my lips as my Mother undoes my chinos. I lift my hips as she pushes them down her fingers caress my skin. My eyes close in defeat.

I am delusional that world has gone along with the men that populated it. Now almost everything including the ocean is toxic to someone like me. As it was toxic to those males after the contraceptive catastrophe. According to my guardians all I would find is a slow, painful death after I had been raped and tortured by the remaining contaminated population.

'Oh, come on, Adam, there are still plenty of women out

there with more money than sense. And who wouldn't want to buy a Lil' cutey like you, huh... coochie coo.' She jokes, pulling at my cheek.

'Ah stop.' I laugh, pushing her hand away, mock scowling.

'Now come on, let's stop messing around and let me get this sample so we can both get on with our day,' she says, suddenly all business again.

'Alright fine,' I agree my tone petulant, but I don't care as I settle back and prepare myself.

So here I am, lying on the couch, while a stunningly attractive woman strokes and coaxes me to perform, so she can collect my sample.

'Oh, you are a good boy,' she coos, as I pick up my book to distract myself from what she's doing.

'Well done, sweetheart.' She bends and kisses my forehead, as I try my level best to focus on my book.

In my mind, this was my last chance at convincing The Genetic Corporation not to retire me. As far as I could see, this was the tipping point. There is no other option for me now than to leave. If I stay, I will spend the next three years being milked until I reach twenty, then I will either be euthanised or sold to become some woman's plaything. Of course, they will sterilise me first. When she tires of me, she will be in her right to have me put to sleep, euthanised, legally killed. They want us young, fresh and easy to control. So, to avoid that I am willing to take my chances against the toxin and escape.

My belly tightens with the pleasure that washes over me; the sample collected. Heat steals up my cheeks as disgust fills me. Laying back as she cleans me up. Adjusting my clothing, she packs the jars away ready to be processed and sent to the laboratory.

'Adam sweetheart, it will be alright,' my eyes snap open.

'How can it be?' My abrupt reply. She shrinks back, her

hand still on my thigh. 'If I am lucky, depending on how you view these things, I will be genetically matched. The girl will be given papers for me, and I will become her property and expected to breed with her,' my voice louder than normal.

'Adam...' I hold my finger up to stop her interruption I know what she will say. Frankly, I don't want to hear it.

'Once she has a baby,' I continue. 'She doesn't have to keep me. She can hand me back to be euthanised or she can sell me. So yeah, what can I say? I don't want any of that. Who would!' I close my eyes again and I wait for her answer. With a sigh, I relax my body. Her hand is rubbing my thigh to comfort me. It is against regulations for her to show any affection.

'Adam, please, you can't dwell on that. You must live the life you have.' Sitting up, I brush her hand off my leg and do my trousers up.

'I can't. You know I am not like the other Adams. They didn't tamper with my DNA and dumb me down. Make me docile,' lurching to my feet, I move to the window and watch the boys playing in the snow. Mathew waves and I wave back. I know when she is behind me.

'Adam, I know the mistakes they made with you. How you miss Aaron since he died? They should never have let either of you develop naturally. Gen—Corp won't euthanise you just because you are different.' Her hand is on my waist as she breaks the rules and hugs me. I turn to her and hang my head so she can't see my expression.

'Sorry, you are right. I should forget about my future and live in the now.' Some dark part of me wants to give in let them euthanise me. Join Aaron. The other part of me wants to live. Leave this place and see the world. Find my own girl to fall in love with. Like in the old days. The only way to achieve that is to escape and next week they move the matched boys out. This is done every six months and I am going to use that to hide my escape.

'Good boy,' she kisses my cheek, another rule broken. 'I will see you at dinner,' she picks up the medical case.

'Yes,' turning I manage a smile. Waiting as she closes the door, leaving me to my thoughts.

Today I am implementing the first part of my plan. Stealing a key card to get out of the house unnoticed. Once I have observed and timed the guard change so I can sneak away. There is a hole in the fence I can use. Well, that's my plan. From there, I will make my way to the town and the station. By the time they notice I am missing, I will be long gone.

I am going to head to Ireland. I read it isn't like here. Because it is an island, it shut its borders. The large catholic population, they didn't implement the new contraceptive for the men. Although they lost their men eventually, like everywhere else, it was slower, and they didn't have the civil unrest that followed the disaster. Which I hope means it is still like the old world.

Some articles I read indicated they had a small population of men, proper men, not like me. That, though, isn't what interests me. Ireland isn't controlled by Gen-Corp. So, in theory, I could be free there. Of course, I am still assuming just being outside won't in fact kill me.

I give it a couple of minutes, then spring to my feet, hastening towards the door and glance into the hallway. As I suspected, it is deserted with everyone distracted by the snowball fight. I make my way down the hallway and up a flight of service stairs at the end of the first-floor landing.

Where the ground floor comprises of leisure and dining space, they split this floor between administrative offices and the Mothers' private quarters. I am not supposed to be up here and will have to answer some pretty troublesome questions if I am caught.

I sneak along the corridor, occasionally peering into the deserted offices or listening for the sound of someone coming. Fortunately, no one is around. I creep along until I find one door to the Mothers' rooms lodged open by some dirty clothes. Even though they are always telling us to be clean and tidy, some of them can be quite messy.

I enter the room like a ninja and start carefully rummaging through the pockets of the discarded clothes, searching for a key card that will allow me to get through one of the external doors into the gardens.

Having no luck amongst the clothes, I turn my attention to the bedside tables, finally finding one under a stack of papers next to the Mother's bed. The doors in and out of the home close and lock automatically and I would never escape unless I had one of these key-cards to open them again.

Successful, I exit the room, careful to leave it in a similar state to the way I found it. I hurry along the landing and down the stairs to the ground floor, the key-card safely stuffed in my pocket, and back towards the drawing room where I had been reading.

I re-entered the room to find my Mother there waiting for me. 'Sweetheart, where have you been? I thought you were reading your book?' A look of curiosity came upon her face, my book in her hand.

'Adam, why didn't you join in with the other boys today?'

She looks at me, waiting. A sigh escapes my lips. 'I don't know. I wanted to but… I just I had a lot on my mind I guess,' giving a shrug again, this time trying not to give anything away under her scrutiny. 'I had my art lesson,' I shrug.

'That was only an hour you could have joined in after,' she looks at me with a puzzled expression and I realise she doesn't understand me at all. With a frown I drop my gaze.

'Oh, Adam, you worry too much. You are a good boy and always have been. You need to forget all this nonsense about retiring and just enjoy the time you have.' She pulls me to her and links her arm with mine. Hugging me into her side as we walk along the corridor. What is it with her and hugging? I glance at her; she can never understand how frightened and trapped I feel. The numb feeling that has replaced the sadness at this realisation settles around me, within me.

'Why make me like this? Why give me this intelligence? What is it for? Why didn't they make me docile like the other boys, though? There must be a reason?' It all blurts out the frustration of my situation and her. She won't ever understand.

'Enough Adam. Please sweetheart, trust me. I will find you a good match and you will have an enjoyable life. Alright.' I glare at her before walking away. 'Adam, honey, the world isn't a safe place for you. Just stop with all the questions, I have it organised,' she searches my face, waiting for my compliance. That can't be the reason or am I deluding myself. Only one way to find out, leave and see for myself.

* * *

A CACOPHONY of noise assaults my ears as I enter the dining room. I stop to take in the ornate plaster and freezes that decorate the walls. The stately home that we live in, with its grand elegant decorations taken from a bygone age, never fails to amaze me. It's such a calm, refined contrast to the chaos and drama of its residents, as the boys boisterously eat their dinner. Mother kisses me on the cheek before walking across the polished wooden floor to the table that all the Mothers sit at.

The delicious scent of roast chicken dinner wafts around me, causing my stomach to growl. Dodging the kitchen and dining staff bustling around the room clearing plates and already bringing out dessert, I make my way past the rows of tables, each packed with boys of varying ages chattering and eating their dinner. Finding my place, pleased to see my dinner already on the table. Taking my seat, I listen to the conversation going on around me as they discuss the snowball fight; I smile at their boyish enthusiasm.

'You're very quiet,' Mathew nudges me as I fork a roast potato. Popping it into my mouth. His intense green eyes watch my every move. I feel heat warm my cheeks at his scrutiny.

'Adam, are you still worrying about me going?' He asks as I eat my potato.

'Yeah, I guess.'

'I will be fine. Mother has a match for me,' he beams at me. His statement should have been a surprise, but in all honesty, Mathew should be the poster boy for The Adam Program. Someone was really paying attention when they created him. He really is beautiful, and it isn't just physical, he is just a nice person.

'Really? Who?' Swallowing my food, I turn to look at him. How can he be so accepting? Oh, yeah, he was made to be.

'I don't know but she is high ranked,' an enormous grin on his face. 'So, I will be fine little dude.' chuckling he ruffles my hair.

'Get off.' I push his arm away and straighten my hair, glaring at him as he laughs.

'You are so grumpy today.'

'Yeah, sorry, tired I guess,' I answer. Finishing my dinner, I gaze at my pudding, chocolate sponge and custard; I don't fancy it and push it away. I don't like this stodgy food. My mother has a device that I like to watch old cooking shows on. Fantasies of strolling around a market, choosing the ingredients before spending the day creating a delicious meal. Inviting friends around to share it. Like people used too before the disaster and civil unrest. Before the world changed and Gen-Corp took over. Before all the men died, not like me, but proper men. Like in the cooking shows I enjoy and the books I read.

'Oh, you gonna eat that?' Mathew asks eyeing my pudding pulling me from my musings.

'No, do you want it?' I don't know why I am asking as I know the answer.

'Yes, please.' He pulls the bowl to him and demolishes it. 'Film night tomorrow, are you going?' He asks, pushing the now empty bowl away.

'Oh, yes,' my reply filled with enthusiasm. Film night is one of my few pleasures here. He gets up as his Mother calls him.

'I will come and get you and we can sit together?' He smiles as he leaves with his Mother, one more milking before bed. I sigh and push my chair out, climbing to my feet as my own Mother calls me. Knocking into someone.

'Sorry,' my apology automatic as cutlery clatters to the floor. Immediately I drop to pick it up.

'Please, stop,' a timid voice has me looking up into a pair of pale blue eyes. She reaches out and takes the cutlery from my hand as I rise.

'Sorry,' my smile instant. As a shout comes from across the room. The girl stiffens.

'Audrey,' a plump stern woman strides toward us. 'I must apologise sir she is new,' she grabs the girl's arm and yanks her back. A flash of pain briefly flares on Audrey's face.

'That's alright it was all my fault I wasn't watching where I was going,' my explanation comes as my Mother arrives a frown on her face.

'Come Adam,' leading me away I glance back and see the girl being chastised. Her eyes momentarily lock with mine and I mouth a sorry. A smile flickers across her lips as she is dragged away.

* * *

CLIMBING OUT OF BED, I move to the window, pushing back the curtain, peering outside. The snow has stopped. It is early, just gone five. I have a good couple of hours before breakfast and the first milking. Getting dressed as quickly as I can I do up my chinos and slipping a warm navy sweater over my head. Sitting on my bed, I wriggle on some thick socks and grab my boots, not putting them on.

Moving over to the door of my room, carefully pulling it open, I check the hall. It is deserted; obviously, no other idiot would be up. My feet make no noise on the plush brown carpet as I creep past the other boys' rooms, taking the stairs two at a time. I finally reach the door to the garden and drop my boots to the floor. Pushing my feet inside and doing up the laces. I glance down the hall toward the stairs, checking no one has heard me. No, Mother about to call me back. Reaching into my pocket, I pull out the stolen key card and hold it against the sensor next to the door. After a moment of hesitation, the sensor flashes green, and the door clicks. I reach out my hand, pushing the handle and nudging the door open.

Standing in the doorway inhaling the crisp, fresh air as it fills my lungs. The cold tingles on my skin, the hushed whispering noise that snow seems to make telling the secrets of the things it has buried. I gaze around. No one is about. I know armed guards patrol the perimeter fence, and I'll have to be careful to avoid them if I don't want to get caught.

Taking my first step into the snow, marvelling at the delicious sound it makes as it crunches under my boot. I make my way around the house towards the small wood just on the south side of the fence. Checking I am not being watched, I stay concealed as I watch the guards. Counting how many there are and then I time how long it takes for them to do a perimeter. I need to know this if I am going to get out.

'Adam, what the hell are you doing out here?' Mathew's voice makes me twist. I hadn't heard him as I had been concentrating on the guards.

'No... nothing,' my voice stutters annoyingly, 'I am just enjoying the quiet you know.'

'Oh Adam, are you thinking about Aaron? I know it is coming up to the anniversary.' he moves over to me and puts his arm around me.

'Oh yeah, really miss him, you know, he loved snow,' the lie just seems to glide off my tongue and a bit of me feels bad. I do think about Aaron and miss him enormously, but in this instant, I am not thinking about him.

'How did you get out here?' Looking him over, I notice he isn't properly dressed for this weather. He has his indoor shoes on, not boots like me and he has a hoody on, rather than a coat.

'I um, followed you but lost you when a guard came,' I am not entirely sure that was the truth.

'Come on, it's cold out here,' I take his hand and drag him back inside.

'Where did you get that key card from?' He asks, as I knew he would eventually. Despite his bumbling attitude, Mathew seems to watch everything.

'Mother gave it to me,' I am getting good at this, I congratulate myself, as I lie again. I am going to have to be careful. He will watch me if I know Mathew. I have a quick debate about telling him my plan and then change my mind. He will talk me out of it. I know he would.

CHAPTER 2

'Mathew, you idiot, where are you?' I laugh as I run along the corridor. The boards creak beneath my feet, my rubber bottomed shoes squeaking on the varnished wood; they didn't bother to carpet the attic. To be fair, only Mathew and I come up here.

'In here,' he shouts as I push the door open to find him stood at a window. He doesn't turn as the door bangs shut behind me.

'What you looking at?' I peer over his shoulder, smiling at the view. In the distance, the river snakes through the farmland and further off is the small town that most the staff come from, brought in and out each day under tight security.

'Look at all the people, I have never seen it this busy, not even when...' his voice trails off as he feels me stiffen next to him. 'Sorry!' He drapes an arm around my shoulders and pulls me close.

'It's okay,' but it isn't, not really. I know what he was going to say, and it scares me.

We watch the activity before turning and settling down on the bean bags we dragged up here. I place the board between us and start setting my pieces in their places. I am white and Mathew is black. He watches me smiling as he places his. We both pick up our last pawn together and, laughing at each other, we place them on the board at the same time. Then we sit, contemplating our first moves. My elbows are on my knees as I rest my chin in my hands. Without looking, Mathew is doing the same, his long legs crossed like mine.

'It will be alright.' His gaze locks with mine. 'You know, without me.' He nods as if that is the end of it.

'Yeah, I know,' I say, casting my gaze at the game.

'Time will pass quickly, and we will see each other again, you are bound to be matched to someone important.' He grins and I half smile back.

'What if it's all lies?' I blurt, unable to hold in the nagging doubts.

'What?' He frowns as his fingers hover over his chess piece.

'What if they just say that to keep us here, stop us from freaking out and escaping?' I am slightly annoyed when he laughs.

'Adam, man, you think way too much besides you don't kill your most valuable assets now, do you?'

'I suppose,' I concede and concentrate on the game. Maybe he is right. I try to convince myself, but to me neither option is very appealing. 'But I don't want that. I don't want their plan for me,' I blurt out, unable to look at him.

'What... what do you mean?' he splutters. With a sigh, he settles his gaze on me as I glance at him. 'Adam, mate, what exactly do you want? Maybe if you tell me, we can sort it all out, yeah.' I think about that for a minute, unsure if I should share with him. He is watching me closely in that way he does. Mathew is very observant once you get past his bumbling nature. His expression is one of puzzlement, but his eyes are calculating. Sometimes I don't think Mathew is as he seems. I brush off my misgivings as I marshal my thoughts.

'I want...' I pause.

'Go on,' he encourages.

'I want a puppy,' he looks at me confused, then bursts out laughing.

'Stop it,' I grumble with indignation as he controls his mirth. 'What I meant was I want a house, a home of my own and a pet. Not be someone's pet. I want to choose what I am going to eat and make it myself. Not have someone else's decision thrust upon me.' I run my hand through my hair. 'I want my time to be my own and fall in love properly. Not be matched to a stranger.' I gaze at him to see his reaction and I am shocked to see sadness pulling at his features.

'Adam,' his voice is sombre. 'You know that can never happen, don't you?' his voice is soft as his eyes roam my face. I hang my head in defeat.

'I know,' my voice a petulant mumble. 'But why can't I? There must be somewhere in this vast world where I can have that?' It comes out angry and I see him flinch.

'No, Adam, you can't because the world isn't like the stories in your books, or the programs you like to watch. That has all gone along with the men. You know that as well as I do.' Now he is looking at me with pity, and honestly, I want to punch him.

'Look, just forget I said anything, okay. Check mate,' I push his king down harder than necessary.

'Adam, you need to reconcile yourself with what you are. What we are and our purpose.'

'Then I would rather die,'

'No... No Adam, never say that' his voice aghast.

I pack away the game, sliding the box against the wall as Mathew stretches his cramped muscles. Surging to my feet and stretching my arms above my head, I release the tension in my back from sitting in the same position for so long.

'Time for tea I reckon.' Mathew grabs my arm, pulling me out of the room and along the corridor to the stairs just as my Mother appears. She is dressed down in jeans and a jumper, trainers on her feet.

'Hello, Mother, are you okay?' I ask as we walk along the corridor towards her. 'You look troubled.'

'Yes, I'm fine. What were you two doing up in the attic?' She asks.

'We go up there to play chess,' Mathew answers. 'It is the only place we get any peace and quiet,' a charming smile graces his face as my Mother can't help herself as she succumbs to his innocent charm. Her features that were stern a moment ago soften.

'I see, well you shouldn't really be sneaking off without supervision. From now on we will keep better track of all your movements.' she informs us with an air of finality.

'Oh, why is that?' I ask, attempting to sound only mildly interested.

'If you must know, last night security found a set of footprints through the snow from the house and into the nearby woods. We suspect it was one of the staff, but we can't be taking any chances. As such, from now on, you shall not go unaccompanied. Fortunately, it highlighted a hole in the perimeter fence that has since been repaired. Now come along, it's time for dinner,' she said before turning around and striding off along the landing. We follow her in silence while I mentally kick myself for being stupid enough to leave a trail of snowy footprints.

* * *

CREEPING along the back corridor that the library is on, my only thought is I hope no one else is using it, but since classes have finished for the day, it should be empty. Placing my hand on the heavy wooden doors, I push them open, cringing at the creaking noise they make, amplified by the silence. It becomes apparent that the library is empty, and the lights are turned off. Carefully closing the doors behind me, I leave the lights off as I move deeper into the library to where the computers are.

I spend so much time in here. The darkness is no hinderance. Moving around the ornately carved oak bookcases. My feet make little noise on the wooden block flooring. Laid in an intricate pattern that matches the carving on the bookcases. The large floor to ceiling windows with their cushion filled seating. Allow the moonlight to shed its pale light. Towards the back, where the enormous fireplace gives the room a sumptuous feel with groups of cosy sofas and armchairs. The fire has already been cleaned and laid for the morning. Interspersed between the cosy seating are dark oak tables and the computers.

Hearing voices, my assumption was wrong: someone else is in here. Getting up, I sidle up to one of the large bookcases, using it to shield me as I crouch against it. I glimpse my Mother talking to someone who I can't see. I hear a snatch of conversation pressing tighter to the bookcase as I listen.

'We need to get him away. He isn't coping. We knew this would happen. He isn't like the other boys. He shouldn't be here doing this, and time is running out.' My Mother's voice rises slightly in agitation. I have never known her upset. She is always so cheerful. Sometimes it annoys me, the way she is always smiling and happy, never getting cross.

'I know, Emma, but it took us time to find you. Plans are being made to move him, but we aren't the only ones who know about him. It will be hard getting him out of the country. You don't want them to move him first, and you don't want them to replace you, change his Mother.'

'Mathew is being moved soon. Can't we use that as a distraction and get him out at the same time?'

'That would be really risky. I got confirmation of Mathew's match today.'

'Who is she?'

'Only Madame Ramsbottom's bloody cousin.'

'Will she accompany her? If she sees Adam, she will know exactly what he is?'

'I am aware of that.'

'Are you willing to take that risk?'

'No, of course not, but he is so sad. It's painful to watch. Please hurry, it was bad enough we split them up…,' My Mother paces. 'He talked to Mathew earlier, said he would rather die than carry on as an Adam.' Damn Mathew, you rotten snitch. I frown in annoyance.

'Look, I will see what I can do, what with the break in the other night. Maybe it is time we moved him. Gen-Corp has been pestering me for him anyway as all his sample's fail. They want him with the other one. What did you tell him about his brother?'

'He thinks Aaron is dead. It was the only way to stop the questions.'

'Aaron is fine. Unlike Adam, he is perfectly happy. Gen-Corp has him secure in a facility before they give him back as per the agreement.' I hear their footsteps on the wooden floor, along with the swish of the door opening and closing, indicating I am alone. She lied, she lied, sinking to the floor, resting my head on my drawn-up knees. She lied. He is alive! Oh, how stupid am I? Is the thought that burst into my head. Of course, he is. He was created the one they wanted. I am the extra surprise and inconvenience they didn't know what to do with.

I want to find him is my first thought, see him, hug him again. I am deviating from my original plan. He is distracting me, like he always did when we were children. But I could find him? The little voice in my head whispers its seduction. Yes, I could but first I have to escape here and soon. If they move me again all I have accomplished here will be lost.

Banging my head on my knees before pushing to my feet. I came here for a reason, and I won't get another chance. I move to the tables grouped together on each sits a screen upon a small black box. Pulling out a chair I run my fingers over the small buttons pressing gently. Pulling the keyboard close as I type in the commands. Scanning the room just to check I am still alone, undiscovered.

The Gen-corp logo dances across the screen a bee entwined with the gender symbol of a male. Depicting the thing that doomed us and saved us and enslaved the likes of me. My dark thought as it fades into the background, and I search the table of contents.

I skim over a brief explanation from Gen-Corp. The disaster that created this world, from what I understand, was a gradual thing. So, a lot of things stayed as the world adapted. As the birth-rate dropped, it seems the world prioritised. So, the internet stayed, not like it was, nothing is like it was before, but enough for me to find the information I need. As the men died because of the contraceptive and the way it broke down in the body. The women, the healthy women prioritised the things that needed to function, such as electricity, farming, food production. The Adam programme, me. Then, of course, maintaining a healthy population. Sterilizing the contaminated girls and women although like the men the contraceptive poisoned them. So, they slowly died. The children born to them to sickly to survive caused a medical dilemma and emergency.

Once online, I download a map of the surrounding area.

That way once I leave the home, I'll at least have a vague idea of where I am going. Avoiding the heavily populated areas if I can while finding safe places to spend the nights. I am distracted by a report. Opening it I read. It seems some girls are clean immune to the contaminant and a cataloguing imitative is being rolled out to find them. I read a bit more before I realise, I must focus. I find all this fascinating which considering it traps me is a little weird. Know your enemy Aaron used to say.

Once the map is printed, I move the mouse over admin and look for my Mother's name. I then spend a few minutes working out her password and look for my movement papers. I print these off, they might come in useful. Above my file are Aarons. I open it and study his movement papers. They moved him around a lot after leaving me. He has a match. The last record of him is a facility near Glasgow. Hang on, they will move him again when he is eighteen. I must find him and soon. I print off the address. Closing that, I find the train timetable because Glasgow is as far away as it gets, and I can't walk all the way. I plan to find him and then go to Ireland. I erase any evidence I have used the computer and then turn it off. Folding the map and other information up, I push it into my pocket and leave the library.

CHAPTER 3

The house is quiet as I get dressed and rummage through my cupboard to find my tatty old satchel from when I was moved to this home after Aaron' so called death. Brushing off the dust to peer inside. Oh yuk! I take it over to the bin, tipping out the mouldy contents of a half-eaten sandwich and a sticky lump that may have been a packet of fruit jellies.

Opening the drawer to my bedside cabinet I grab a bottle of water and a bar of chocolate, the food parcel smuggled out of the dining room at teatime along with the map I printed off yesterday evening before I crept into the deserted kitchens and took a large sharp knife. A change of pants and socks, along with a spare shirt, are shoved inside along with my most precious possession, my drawing book, and small art box containing my pencils and water paints. Last a small amount of money I stole from my Mother. It's not much but it's enough. Moving across the room, I look out the window at the snow. It is heavy now. This is my only chance if I want to escape undetected as the snow will hide my footprints.

She has lied about everything; I don't have to have this

life, and once I find Aaron, we will go to Ireland. According to an article I found online, there are people there that help boys like me. No wonder they monitor our every move, restrict our access to computers and the internet. Grabbing the spare blanket from the top of my wardrobe, I zip my jacket up.

I reach the back door to the house without incident, swiping the card over the sensor. The light turns green, but as I push the door open, an alarm goes off. Damn. The flood lights swiftly follow coming on one by one. Briefly immobilised, sweat on my forehead even though my body has turned cold. I haul in a cleansing breath, blowing it out. My legs obey, my brain moving into shadow just outside the light's reach. Somehow sticking to the plan and instead of making for the fence, I hug the walls of the house and make my way around to where I know the tool shed is. Pulling the latch, I slip inside, only just though as it is packed with rusty old lawn mowers with a window on one side and tool bench littered with bits of wood, rusty metal. I carry on past it towards a set of drawers hidden at the back of the shed. Inside the second from the top drawer, I find what I am looking for, a relatively intact pair of wire cutters.

I hear voices; the guards are coming. Instinctively, I drop between the lawn mowers and attempt to crawl under the desk while simultaneously making myself as small as possible. Momentarily, the shed is flooded with torchlight as two security guards peer through the window into the shed. My heart pounds as I am convinced that they can see me.

'It's empty. Come on, they are by the back fence, I'm telling you.' The guards move on, and I am plunged into darkness. I wait still for a moment in case they come back, and then climb to my feet and leave the tool shed.

If they are going to the back fence, then I will have to escape out of one of the other sides. Fortunately, the snowstorm has gotten worse, and visibility is down to less than five meters now. I cut my way through the fence without incident and squeeze through; unfortunately, the woods that would cover my escape are at the back of the house, while I find myself now stood at the edge of an open field. They will catch me out here, running along the edge of the fence and into the woods.

* * *

A HAND GRABS ME, pulling me against a tree. The suddenness of the action stops me from resisting.

'Damn it, I knew it was you,' my Mother glares at me. 'Who else would hack my account?' Seeing her sad and mostly annoyed expression, my apology is on the tip of my tongue. Until my indignation barrels forward.

'You have been lying to me.' Accusation wraps around every syllable.

'For your own good, why couldn't you just accept everything?'

'Who in their right mind would accept their imminent demise?' hissing that sentence out between my teeth as anger seeps into my stance.

'Oh Adam,' she sighs, I may have won this argument. Now I must persuade her to let me go. That may not be as easy.

'I am not going back,' straightening my spine and pushing back my shoulders, trying to use my height advantage.

'Don't be ridiculous, you have no idea how much danger you are in out here,' her gaze is unwavering, despite the twitch under her eye. Aaron and I called it her mad witch twitch.

'Well, explain it to me why don't you, all this danger, most the population is now sterile, so I am no use to them, am I. If I should come across a girl, I could make babies with, she will be more cautious than me, won't she? In case Gen-Corp catches her and used her in one of the breeding programs. Or was that all a lie as well?' my tone is challenging as I wait for her answer, one I know she won't give me.

The sound of a twig breaking has my Mother swinging around, pushing me to the ground.

'Emma, what on earth are you doing out here?' A young woman steps out of the tree cover. Pushing the large fur edged hood down, revealing a pretty but ordinary face. Her gaze flicks toward me, then back to my Mother. 'Ah, of course.'

'I could ask you the same thing. Except I know why you are here, and I am not giving him up to you,' Mother lowers her voice as it vibrates with anger.

'Oh Emma, you were always going to hand him to me eventually,' the stranger chuckles.

They stand squaring up to each other, circling a mere arm's length apart. I feel fear creep over me and sweat breaks out over my body, which I could really do without, trying to use the tree to shelter me from the biting wind, watching my Mother, as I climb back to my feet.

'Come on Emma, would you really threaten me?' I see something glint in the moonlight.

'To keep him safe. Yes, I would'

'He would be safe with me after all I have had custody of the other one for years.'

'In a medical facility. Experimented on like a glorified lab rat. They are people like us, children, not bartering chips,' my Mother replies, knife clutched in her hand.

'That was always your flaw. You care too much. He is just another commodity,' the other woman jeers as she walks towards me. Hauling me roughly forward, taking my chin in her fingers, she turns my head to study me. I scowl at her, and she smiles at me, but it's not a friendly smile.

Taking in her features, the first thing that amazes me is she is young, I mean really young, not much older than me. The next is she is plain, not beautiful, her features aren't perfect, she has glasses on, which suggests to me they have not tampered with her DNA.

'He is pretty, I give you that. They will pay for these looks. His genetics are exemplary. Even his daughters will be attractive, never mind the sons and of course he was the first. They will even pay to sleep with him and to be impregnated naturally,' she laughs. Can't say I found any of that amusing.

'No, that wasn't the deal you promised. If you go back on it, I will kill him.' Mother grabs me and holds the knife to my throat. The other woman chuckles. I still don't find any of this funny.

'Don't be ridiculous,' she pulls me away from Mother and runs her hands over me, touching me. Is he a good boy, obedient?' Her hand is between my legs, and I feel repulsed and nauseated by her. This is not funny. 'Of course, he isn't. Running away was he. Tut tut, what a naughty boy,' she says this with a twinkle in her eye and a smirk on her lips. It takes all my training not to smirk back. Already this stranger has a measure of me. Am I that easy to read?

'Get away from him,' my Mother pushes her away. I stumble and fall to the ground. I see a flash of silver and my Mother gasps before stepping forward, her hand with the knife in between them. They seem to hug, and I frown at such odd behaviour after their argument. The other woman sags and Mother lets her drop to the floor. She turns to me and looks me over as she pulls me up and into a hug.

'Are you alright Adam?' She hugs me tight. 'Come on, we need to get you away from here. More will follow.' She takes my hand and leads me through the wood to the meadow. I crane my neck and look back. The person is still laid in the snow unmoving, and it is then I realise Mother has killed someone. I swallow and allow Mother to drag me through the wood.

'Is she dead?'

'No, good grief, what sort of person do you think I am?'

'Well... I don't know any more.'

'Adam, I am here for you, that's my job, you.'

'You aren't taking me back?'

'No, not right now. That option has gone now. What was your plan? I assume you have one,' I hesitate for a split second, as the voice in my head reminds me. She lied.

'To find Aaron' she laughs. Bloody hell, yeah, I am offended.

'There is a cave on the other side of the river. You go there and wait for me, understand. I can get you back in tonight.'

'I am not going back.'

'Look, you stupid idiot, you will die out here.

'I will die in there, so that argument is redundant. I would rather die out here on my terms than be euthanized on a stranger's whim.'

'Just go to the cave, Adam,' she sighs out as the trees creak under the weight of the snow.

CHAPTER 4

Once through the woods, I come to the edge of another meadow. It is a sea of white and I can just make out the river snaking on its course, steam drifting into the air above it. Where's the bridge that crosses the river? The snow, although falling more softly now, is thick, making me lift my feet higher with each step as I sink almost to my knees. My trousers cling to my legs coated in snow, numbing my legs. I can't feel my fingers from the cold. Dogs are barking and people shout in the woods behind me.

My heart hammers as I attempt to run through the field. The voices get closer as torchlight reflects off the snow at the edge of the wood. I can see the bridge now and desperately urge my aching legs forward to what I hope will offer me some respite from this energy-sapping cold. I know where the cave is. I had already marked it on my map. Initially, it hadn't been my intention to go there, as it is too obvious. The first place they would look, but with the cold sapping my energy. I need somewhere to warm up and plan my next move. I will not wait around for her. That decision has already been made.

Getting to the bridge, I grip at the handrail and draw in a breath, feeling the tingle on my teeth from the frigid air. I wipe away the snot and tears on the sleeve of my jumper and try to get my bearings, a numb feeling growing in the pit of my stomach as the realisation that I am on my own for the first time in my life sets in. My mouth turns up into a smile as I wrapped my arms around myself in a hug. Yeah, that is how pleased I am with myself. Until the sound of the dogs barking pulls me back to my immediate predicament and the cold.

Having crossed the bridge, I come to the cliff face, searching along it, frantically looking for the entrance to the cave. Stopping outside, I can hear voices. What the hell. Have security got here already? No, I would have seen them, and they would have seen me. Dismissing that idea and proceeding with caution, I enter the cave, pulling up my hood to conceal my face. Strolling in like this is normal, avoiding eye contact with the women inside. I soon realise they are mostly the staff from the home. Damn, looking down, making it harder to see my face. I recognise the second chef and two maids from my floor. This many women in one place surrounding me are unnerving.

'Hey, girl, is the snow still bad?' Damn, she is talking to me.

'Yes, erm, it is deep now,' squeaking my voice to sound more like a female, shuffling away, quite glad of my feminine stature for once. The cave is outstanding. If this wasn't such a life and death situation, I would explore all of this thoroughly. The ceiling soars far above my head and strips of crystal sparkle in the walls. In places, you can clearly see the different layers of sediment laid down to make the rock walls. Giving it an unreal, ethereal ambiance.

In the centre of the vast rock cavern, a fire has been lit the flames, causing shadows to dance on the walls all around.

Heat, a welcomed relief to the biting cold. I make my way to the back, but near enough to the fire to benefit from its heat.

'What are you doing here?' Her voice pulls me to a stop. Her hand goes to my hood.

'Please don't,' I whisper.

'What are you doing here? Are you the reason the alarms are going?'

'N... no,' I stutter. 'Please just let me go,' I beg.

'You won't survive out here you should go back,' she whispers back.

'Audrey, who are you talking to get over here now girl,' She looks up biting her lip. She turns back to me.

'I will let you go, but please when the snow stops go back,' she pleads letting go of me and walking toward a group. I recognise some of them from the dining room.

The adrenalin has worn off now and my body just feels numb and tired, so tired. My clothes are slowly drying, and the shivering has stopped, thank goodness. Now is the time to plan. Staying here isn't an option, if I don't want to go back and I can categorically say I am not waiting for my Mother and security. Rummaging in my bag for the map, I am so distracted by this that I almost fail to notice a new woman enter the cave and would have, were it not for the commotion her horse caused as she leads it into the cave with her.

Her piercing green eyes scan the cave, then settle on me, like she can see right through the blanket and knows exactly who and what I am. Butterflies fill my stomach as our eyes lock, and I instinctively understand that she knows. I train my eyes on her, unable to look away while she ties the horse up and talks to it.

Turning from the horse, she walks directly toward me. Sweat runs down my neck, familiar fear grips me, and I feel physically sick, knowing there is nothing I can do that will stop her progress toward me. I can't run, people will notice me. Instead, I reach slowly into my bag and wrap my fingers around the large knife hiding in there. Paralysing fear glues me to my place as she sits down next to me.

'It isn't safe here. The Security will find you. In a minute, I will get up and leave. You will wait a couple of minutes and then follow me, okay? Nod if you understand.' I shake my head vigorously, scowling at her.

'I don't know you. Why should I trust you?'

'You don't have to trust me; you just have to be smart enough to realise that you have a choice. You can stay here in this cave and be caught or killed. Continue going it alone and get lost in the storm right before you die of hypothermia. Or you can come with me, and you might actually make it to freedom,' she pauses. 'Alive,' her voice devoid of emotion.

With the full gravity of my situation laid out before me, I realise that maybe going with her wouldn't be such a bad idea. Besides, I wasn't relishing the thought of travelling alone.

'How do I know you are not from the home?' Glancing around, wary that the other people in the cave could listen in on our conversation.

'If I was with The Genetic Corporation, don't you think that I would have bought their security with me or gone and got them as soon as I saw you, Adam?' She replies and I can't tell if she knows my name or is just saying what I am for effect.

'Alright fine, I'll meet you by the old oak in the field east of here in twenty minutes,' I reply, as she climbs to her feet.

'Make it ten,' she commands as she walks towards the mouth of the cave. She is stopped on the way by a skinny, underfed, dark-skinned girl.

'Celina girl, where did you get that fancy horse?' The skinny girl runs her hand over the horse's flank.

'I got that job. He comes with it.' She is lying, the smile on her face is forced, not reaching her eyes. 'I was running an errand when I got caught in this storm,' she adds holding eye contact with the girl, as she draws herself up, her body language now confident. The other girl seems to shrink a bit.

'That we all did,' the skinny girl replies, as nods and murmurs of agreement echo around the cave.

'Security are coming, it isn't safe in here,' Celina says raising her voice so that everyone in the cave can hear her.

'How you know that?' A woman shouts from by the fire.

'I heard their dogs. I came in here to warn you all, that big house with the high fence, its searchlights are on, and its sirens are going off,' she says, turning back to her horse.

'We can't go out there. It's a white-out,' someone else complains.

'Better that than dying in here,' she answers flippantly, and a murmur goes around the cave.

'That place housed Adams. The only reason the alarms would go off is if one of them escaped. We should hunt it and sell him.'

'Do you think one has escaped?'

'Worth a fortune they are. We could keep him, use him and then sell him.'

What the hell? Carefully, I pull the blanket, so it conceals me some more.

'What, and get shot when we get caught with one?'

'Better than getting shot in here!' Murmurs go around the cave as I shrink further into my blanket.

My attention returns to the red-haired girl, Celina, the skinny girl called her. As she unties her horse and leads it outside. I wait a while as a small procession of people who have taken heed of her warning leave the cave.

ADAM

I take my map out and try to figure out my bearings before climbing to my feet and making my way to the entrance of the cave. I can feel the eyes of the five people that remain upon me, including the girl that had spoken to Celina.

CHAPTER 5

The snow is coming down harder now, and it is hard to see where I need to go. Eventually, though, the old oak comes into view along with Celina and her horse.

'Are you alright? Are you hurt?' My teeth are chattering so much that it is easier to just nod. The dogs are close, their incessant barking the only sound over the wind, torch light on the bridge.

'No, I am not hurt,' I stutter through chattering teeth.

'Good, now get on the horse,' she commands. My obedience automatic, damn it. She pulls my blanket tighter around me and wraps her arm around my waist. I'm not used to being touched by strangers and flinch. If she notices, she doesn't say. She fusses a bit more getting comfortable with me pulled into her front.

'Done,' it comes out sharp. She huffs with annoyance behind me.

'Yes, thank you,' she grumbles, and I can't help but smile.

She walks the horse deeper into the wood. The dogs and torch light are very close, but the overgrown wood, with its straggly trees and weed shrubs, obscure us from view. Snow is falling so thickly our hoof prints disappear faster than we made them as the storm swallows us. The last sound I hear is a popping noise followed by screaming. The girl kicks the horse into a gallop. Screaming fades and hunching tighter into my blanket, I dip my head to combat the snow and cold.

* * *

AFTER WHAT FEELS like a long time, she slows the horse from the crazy speed we were doing to a gentle trot. My eyelids get heavy as the cold sucks all my energy. Jerking awake, I notice she is talking and try to get my cold, sluggish brain to register what she is saying. I notice for the first time her voice is different to mine. Yeah, I know she is a girl – I mean her vowels are soft rounded and quite pleasant to listen to.

'Hey Thom, I have a boy, young, not retirement age. Yes, alright, no, he isn't mine. The place was on lockdown, sirens going the works, security everywhere. Okay, will do that, talk to you later, bye.'

'Who was that' I slur.

'You need to stay awake,' she pulls me into her tighter.

'C ... cold,' I shiver.

* * *

SOMEONE IS RUBBING ME VIGOROUSLY; she has removed my boots and wet trousers.

'Come on wake up,' someone is pulling my damp cold clothes off. 'Oh, I don't want to do this,' feeling of warm skin makes me open my eyes. I am rolled in a blanket with the girl, and we are both wearing very little. It is very snug and warm. She is sort of curled around me.

'I am awake,' I mumble into her shoulder.

'Thank goodness,' she moves away, and I immediately

miss her warmth. She pulls a shirt over my head it is warm and smells of her.

My gaze travels around the building we are in. It is basic and stacked with very large round straw bales. I have never seen anything like this and run my fingers over the rough golden straw. We are tucked between two tall stacks. It is relatively warm in here, shielded by the straw out of the biting wind which I can hear howling around us. I scoot away from her, pulling the blanket tight around me.

'Thank you.' She ignores me and rummages in her large bag before throwing a pair of jeans at me. Catching them, I pull them on. She looks at me and sighs, before getting up and seeing to her horse.

The jeans are an odd fit and I guess they are hers. My attention now caught by her horse. I have only seen pictures of horses so to see one up close is thrilling. 'That's a nice horse. I've never seen one up-close before,' I remark. It is quite a magnificent horse, its coat a deep chestnut brown with a white patch on its face and feet. 'Can I touch him?' I pull my dry seater on from my bag and rummage to find dry socks.

'Sure,' I scramble to my feet and tentatively edge close to the horse. It turns to look at me as I swallow. It is huge.

'He won't bite you,' I glance at her as I edge closer to the horse. 'Hold your hand out flat for him to sniff,' she instructs watching me with amusement.

I do as she instructs. Slowly, I reach out my hand and touch its nose. My fingers run over the velvet softness. A smile pulls at my lips as I glance at the girl, she is building some sort of nest with the straw.

'What's its name?' I have run my hand along his neck and smile as it nudges me with its nose. His soft hair against my fingers. He smells all earthy and a bit like the girl.

'His name's Bob,' she replies. Her short red hair is poking

out from under her woollen hat, and occasionally she glances at me as she rubs Bob down. She has removed his saddle and is rubbing him with an old towel. Moving away to sit down amongst the straw, my gaze strays to her.

'Why didn't you give me back?'

She finishes with the horse and sits next to me, pulling a blanket around her. She shuffles closer and I try not to flinch as her shoulder brushes against mine. Passing her one of my sandwiches, I return her smile before biting into it, cheese.

'Why would I do that? You heard them. You are very valuable,' she smirks at me as I try not to choke on my sandwich.

'Why were you there?' She is lying. I heard her talking. She was there to collect someone.

'That Adam is none of your business.'

'It is if you are going to sell me. Not that I will allow you to do that,' I growl at her, trying my best to be intimidating.

'How are you going to stop me?' In a split second she has me pinned against a bale. My arm twisted behind my back. 'I could kill you now and no one would know,' she whispers in my ear, pushing my arm higher, making me quiver with pain. 'I could have killed you earlier when you were unconscious. Or used you, your body so well trained it doesn't need you awake,' she smirks as I blush. 'Fortunately, you are more useful alive, and I like my partners to participate,'

'No... NO!' I shout through the pain. 'No, you won't kill me.' With strength I didn't know I had; I push her away. Forcing her to the ground, I have my knife in my hand at her throat. 'I am not something you can do with as you please, I am a person,' I seethe climbing off her walking away. I find a crevice between the large round bales, wrapping my blanket around me I do my best not to cry at her meanness. She glances at me and then bursts out laughing.

'Wow, how did you survive the Adam program with that temper?' She shakes her head. 'It might save your life,' she moves next to me, pulling her blanket around us, creating a warm nest. 'Look sorry, okay,' her mirth still evident.

'Apology accepted.' I glare at her.

'We'll stay here for a bit until the storm passes. Thank you for the sandwich.' she wiggles about getting comfortable. As she gazes at me again with her piercing green eyes. 'I won't touch you, promise. You can sleep,' Nodding, I pull my hood up and close my eyes. I don't talk; in all honesty, I have no idea what to say. Her capability is intimidating. I suspect I won't get the upper hand again.

CHAPTER 6

I am startled awake as an elbow jabs my ribs and instinctively grab my knife. My eyes scan the barn, but only the girl is there. She smiles at me and carries on folding her blanket. Putting my knife down, I pull my boots on. Yuk, they are damp and cold. She walks over to me and gently wraps a blanket around my shoulders. I don't mean to, but I flinch at her touch again, blushing I cast my eyes down.

It is still dark, but I notice the quiet as the wind has dropped, indicating the storm has passed. Glancing at my watch, tiredness still tugging at me, its luminous hands read it's just past four am.

'Adam it is still very cold, but I will get us somewhere warm as soon as I can, okay?' Her voice startles me, her eyes sweeping my body checking me over. A blush heats my cheeks at her piercing gaze; turning away, I place my icy hands on them to cool them down so she can't see the effect she has on me. I'm still unsure of whether she knows my name.

'Yes,' coughing to clear my throat, feeling heat creep up

my cheeks. How pathetic. She steps closer, her eyes on my face. Meeting her gaze, I can't look away. 'I will be fine now I have dry clothes,' I reassure.

'You are so beautiful,' her voice comes out as the barest whisper as her hand comes up to touch my face. My feet move me back, just out of reach, breaking the spell. She looks me over once more.

'A bit of a shambles and quite dishevelled but beautiful none the less,' turning she returns her attention to the horse.

'Wow, somewhere in that I thought you might have been paying a compliment, but I guess I was wrong,' A wiry smile pulls at my mouth. As she glances at me rolling her eyes in a childish way.

'Please,' she mutters.

'Still gonna sell me?'

'Maybe,' I shake my head. Picking up my knife and slinging my bag over my head, I am still grinning. She gives me a boost up onto the horse and jumps up behind me, urging the horse forward as she does. The snow has nearly stopped, and the wind has dropped, but I still feel cold and so hungry, hopefully, we will go somewhere with food soon. We seem to have reached some sort of amicable companionship. Like a truce has been reached.

'Where are we going?' Looking around, the rolling fields of the countryside have given way to abandoned industrial units, indicating we are getting closer to the town. It's one thing to read about the devastation that occurred after the contraceptive disaster and the civil unrest that followed but to see it. Well, that's a whole different thing. Unfortunately, it only distracts me from my hunger for a short time. 'I'm hungry!' It comes out in a moan. There is no stopping the blush on my cheeks as I realise, I said that out loud.

'We need to pick up some things and then I will get something for us to eat alright,' she gazes at me a moment, her look soft as she smiles. Why is she looking at me like that?

'Um, What,' I enquire as her usual smirk graces her lips. I run my hand through my hair checking for straw.

She shrugs, 'I can't get over how pretty you are,' she says still smirking.

'Thanks, like no one has told me that before, ever,' I huff annoyed.

'And there it is again,' she shakes her head. 'How did you hide that attitude in the Adam program?'

'With skill and panache,' I snap back, and she bursts out laughing.

'No wonder you ran. If you stayed much longer, they would have euthanised you,'

'Well thanks for that reminder of how my life sucks,' I can't help it and a chuckle escapes me.

She steers Bob toward a derelict camping and outdoor store; I frown, wondering why she would bring me here. Half the building has collapsed. Around it, other buildings are in a similar state. No longer needed as the work force diminished and non-essential jobs ceased. Taking in my surroundings the buildings fascinate me as I try to imagine how they might have been.

'Adam, stop loitering and get in here before someone see's you,' her voice annoyed as I push the door open. Stepping inside cobwebs brush my face, making me shiver. The floor is strewn with rubbish. I spot Celina as she walks between the bare aisles towards a door at the back of the store.

I gaze around, fascinated. I have never been in a shop and although the shelves are empty, just covered in dust and debris, I can picture in my head how it was. This remnant of the world before. Now only found in books.

'Adam, come on,' she hisses at me. My daydream ending abruptly as I move to catch her up.

'Why are we here? This place is empty?' I grumble annoyed she has caught me daydreaming – again.

'Because every woman and her daughter are out looking for you and I don't fancy getting caught, so we need some supplies,' her muttered response does little to hide her annoyance.

'What sort of supplies?'

'A tent and something warm for a start, it's blooming freezing.'

'I hate camping,' I mutter. She smirks at me.

'Yeah, me too,' she confesses, and I can't help but chuckle. We seem to have formed some sort of friendship. She pulls out the gun holstered at her hip and carefully turns the handle of a door at the back of the shop. She slowly pushes it open and enters the room, weapon raised. 'Come in, Adam, it's all clear,' she says, and I follow her. It looks like it used to be the shop's office, as there is a desk in the middle of the room with a chair behind it. It's what's in the room's corner that captures my attention, though. Piled in the corner area tent and sleeping bags and clean sets of winter clothes.

'Where did all this come from?' Peering around, I can't help but check we are alone here.

'Some friends of mine left it for us. Stop gawping and help me carry it back to Bob,' she replies as we pick up the supplies and carry them back through the abandoned store and outside to where Bob waits. She fastens the tent and sleeping bags to Bob; she doesn't ask for my help and I don't offer any.

We climb back on the horse and head deeper into the town, which appears mostly abandoned. As we get closer to the centre, it becomes obvious that at least some people still live here as I sometimes catch glimpses of figures moving about and we occasionally pass a tethered horse. We approach a garish one-storey building, which I assume is a restaurant, as there are posters of food in the windows. The girl helps me down off Bob and then grabs a couple of bags we had taken from the camping store; she then turns her attention to me.

'You look a lot like a girl,' she mutters as she messes my hair up, pulling it forward. She is so close to me I can see the freckles dusting her nose. I inhale her scent. She smells like Bob. I try my best not to flinch or push her hand away. 'Just don't talk too loud, you have a deep voice for such a small person,' she smirks at my scowl as I take offence. I'm not small. I am taller than you, I think. I huff and follow her inside, my hands jammed into my trouser pockets.

Glancing around, noise and the delicious smell of food cooking overwhelms my senses. The bright walls and furniture, all in primary colours, are frankly outstanding. This place is amazing. A fast food restraunt. Never in my wildest dreams did I think I would get to visit one of these. So far it is living up to my expectation with its bright interior and the smell of cooking. People bustle about, laughing and talking. What if someone notices I am an Adam? My only thought to dampen my mood.

None of the women in here pay me any attention as they chatter while eating. So, I relax a little, trying to blend in as I saunter through the rows of tables. On closer inspection, I notice there are no children. I know breeding is heavily controlled, but I expected to see a couple. Maybe they are too precious to be in a place like this. I don't expect to see any men and I am correct in that assumption; I am the only one.

Making my way to a bright red plastic table that is vacant in a corner, secluded enough that I can relax. Sitting down and shuffling along a red bench seat. All the furniture seems to be moulded to the floor. Part of me wonders how clean the place is, and another part of me is so hungry I don't care. My gaze just drinks it all in. From the bright lighting to the large posters advertising the food. Such a contrast from the abandonment I have witnessed on my way here.

I wonder where all the people have come from. Vehicles are expensive and a rarity, a luxury few can afford or maintain. So, walking or horses the primary form of transport, I only noticed a few outside as Celina tied up Bob. I know this as cars were a particular fascination for Mathew. I make a mental note to ask Celina.

I pick up the plastic-coated menu and marvel at the choice. Most of which I do not know what it is or what it might taste like. I know what a burger is, but I have never had anything as fancy as this. Part of me would like nothing better than to try everything.

Celina comes back carrying a tray. She places it on the table and passes me a small box, something wrapped in paper, along with some chips and a drink.

Pulling the paper off, I find a burger inside. Hunger takes over and I more inhale the burger than eat it. Never ever been this hungry before. Looking up, I see her smirking. Lowering my gaze, I open the box she gave me finding another bigger burger inside.

'Where are the children?'

'What do you mean?'

'In here, there aren't any children?'

'These people can't afford children Adam. They won't be clean enough. They will be contaminated. The contaminated aren't allowed to breed, they are sterilised. You know that don't you?'

'Oh,' I go back to eating, thinking about what she has just said. Yes, I knew that. Just – I thought. Well, I don't know what I thought. These huge assumptions could get me killed or worse, that is obvious to me now.

'Where have they come from?'

'Who?'

'The people,'

'Oh, um, there is a facility near here. I think I don't know what it manufactures though,' she dismisses my question with a shrug.

'You are clean, aren't you?' I meet her gaze with my next burning question. She, I am sure is one of those girls I read about. We were trained to please or she would be part of the surrogate system.

'Yes.'

'I don't want to make babies with you, is that okay?' I watch for her reaction and am understandably relieved when she smiles.

'That's okay, I don't want a baby with you, or anyone right now.' We eat in comfortable silence, even though I don't look at her I can feel her eyes on me.

'Adam, out here it isn't just about babies, sex is the dominate motive in taking you, but people are poor, really poor and you well....' she looks at me a sadness in her eyes. 'You are so valuable,' she shrugs. 'Some families they have girls that could breed with you,' she trails off. When she said families, I think she was trying to make it sound nicer. It wouldn't be nice I know that.

'I... the thing is that is always my fate, out here or in the home.' shrugging, I go back to my food. What else is there. To them, I am just a commodity, not a person. Something to buy and throw away when they are tired of me. As sad as that is, it is my reality and right now, I don't know if I can escape it. But I want to so desperately it hurts to just think about.

'I just wanted you to be aware of the dangers, that's all,' her eyes skim over me and then settle on my face. 'You are too delicate for here,' her voice quiet and sad.

'I know,' in my head I want to smile, but my face won't cooperate. Turning my attention back to my food. Careful as

I remove the box from the second burger. The big one, this thought, cheers me slightly.

'Hungry, were you?' She raises an eyebrow as I grin through a mouthful of burger. She studies me as she chews slowly.

'Yeah, you could say that' I manage between gulping down one mouthful and going in for another.

'I didn't know what you would like, so I got you the same as me.'

'I don't know what I like here either, but this is nice.'

'Are you telling me you have never been in a burger bar?' She stares at me for longer than I feel is polite. She must know all this stuff, aren't they taught how to take care of us.

'Um, we aren't allowed out, so yeah, I have not been in a burger bar,' I reply, taking another bite out of my burger. 'I have seen pictures and we have burger nights sometimes. It's not like this though.'

'You look cute when you smile, you have dimples, how old are you, fourteen?' Meeting her gaze, I stop chewing and swallow to answer.

'Um, no, I am seventeen,' I reply. Noticing a bit of sauce, I lick it off my finger while watching her delicately eat her burger.

'How old are you?' I ask, partly curious and partly trying to size her up.

'Nineteen, you're not very big for seventeen,' she cocks her head to one side and studies me. She picks up another fry and eats it. 'It's cos you're pretty and delicate looking,' she finishes.

'I used to get teased about that all the time by the other boys. They used to get me to play the girl if we put on plays. It was awful,' I explain as she grins at me. My features, although perfect, are just too delicate to be described as handsome; I have got used to people commenting on how pretty I am.

'Well, it will make it easier to hide you, at least.' she chews on her burger.

'Why are you helping me again? I don't think that you mentioned it in the cave.'

'No, I didn't,' she replies, her gaze not meeting mine. Should I be worried, she has had opportunity to hand me back to Gen-Corp and hasn't so far. Am I being naïve, trusting her?

'Are you going to dress me up as a girl?' I raise an eyebrow. Her hand flies to her mouth as a chuckle escapes her.

'Maybe. Do you have a problem with that?' She gazes at me quizzically, and I suspect she is laughing at me again. I relax; it's nice talking to her. She is an odd-looking girl. Her most striking feature is her green eyes. They are pure green, not watered down with brown or blue, and she has freckles over her nose. I wouldn't call her beautiful, but she is pretty, I suppose. She isn't engineered like me. She isn't quite perfect enough.

The burgers have taken the edge off my hunger, and it is warm in here; being cold all the time is draining.

'No,' but actually I think I would object to a silly dress, even if it was going to save my life. Maybe keep hold of my masculinity a bit longer. Pushing away the drink that has gone watery, I decide a skirt combo might be all right. Why am I thinking this?

'We should use the facilities while we are here, you know clean up a bit.'

'Why?' It just slips out. She stops what she is doing and looks at me.

'It's quite a way to the house and we have at least one night in the tent.' She says, one eyebrow raised. Oh, do I smell? When she isn't looking, I smell myself. I don't smell that much, so relax. Well, I don't think I do. I mean, I don't smell like I do after playing hockey. Maybe girls have a more acute sense of smell than boys. I decide to go along with what she says, anyway. Pushing back the chair, I climb to my feet, following her into the restroom.

She passes me a waterproof brown coat. It is lovely and warm, it's padded and has a fleece lining that is soft and snug, the hood is fur lined and the whole thing reaches to my mid-thigh, enveloping me in a cocoon like warmth. Zipping it up, I pull the hood up, concealing my face. I fold up my blanket as I don't need it now; I have the coat.

'Your family,' I use her terminology. 'What will they do with me? Do they have girls to breed me with?' I need to know this she isn't my friend, and I would be delusional if I thought otherwise. She turns to me.

'No... well yes but it would be your choice,'

'My choice I doubt that' I see the red stain on her cheeks. So, I am right.

'I mean, the girl would be your choice. Not a stranger,' she pauses. 'Adam, you must understand it is our duty to breed. You won't be sold or euthanised with my people, but you are still a male. A fertile male,' she shrugs her gaze drops from mine. When she looks back at me her features are closed showing no emotion from earlier.

She takes my hand and leads me out of the restaurant, which is now getting busy. I notice some security from Gen-Corp and immediately move closer to her. She squeezes my hand pulling me along.

As we walk towards the exit, two Gen Corp security guards walk in. I freeze, a cold sweat engulfing my body as they walk towards us. Their helmets are off, and they are talking amongst themselves and smiling. For a moment, I think they are going to arrest me, but they walk straight past and head towards the counter.

'Come on, Adam let's go.' The girl hisses, trying to spur me back into action. I walk again when someone taps me on the shoulder from behind.

'Excuse me, ma'am.' I freeze again. Slowly, I turn to meet the security guard's gaze.

'I feel like we've met before. Do I know you from somewhere?' The security guard asks.

'Be cool, I will handle this,' Celina hisses in my ear as I open my mouth to speak. I immediately closed it again and stare at the security guard gormlessly.

'You must be mistaken officer, my friend here is a newly purchased Adam,' Celina says, her tone stern and business-like as she steps between me and the security guard. Around us, the conversation has stopped as eyes watch our interaction.

'I am escorting him to his new Mother,' she continues, her hand drifting to the pistol holstered at her waist.

Their eyes immediately focus on me. I stand as still as I can although the urge to squirm under there gaze is hard to resist. They both appear to relax as they look me over.

'Look at him, I ain't ever seen a boy before,' the shorter one says, stepping nearer me and looking at me closely. I stay still as a sudden movement, and they might shoot me.

'He looks more like a flat-chested girl than a boy,' the other remarks.

'Do you think we should check?' Shorty asks and I swallow not liking that idea.

'Dunno, which part is different,' the other one undoes my coat and shrugs.

'You will not touch him unless A. you have a permit or B. you want me to take this up with your superiors. Who did you say your commanding officer was again?' Celina asks, her tone stern. Both the guard's backup slightly, straightening as their expressions become more serious.

'Show us your papers and his movement orders,' the taller one commands. Once they find out we have no documentation, this will be over quickly. I stand nervously, my head bowed, hands behind my back as I have been taught, a display of submission.

'Here,' I almost bring my head up in shock and it takes all my training not to.

The shorter guard takes the papers from the girl's hand and spends some time looking them over.

'These seem in order,' Shorty says as she hands them back. 'I need to catalogue his number.'

'Of course,' the girl takes my arm with the tattoo on it and Shorty runs her scanner over it.

'These are dangerous times. You should have more protection with you.' The other says, still gazing at me with a hungry look that I really don't like. It makes me nervous.

'That encourages too much attention; besides this one is so pretty. He looks like a girl,' as she takes my chin and shows them my face. It takes an enormous amount of willpower not to react.

'Indeed, he does,' the security snigger as Celina takes my hand and pulls me away.

'You take care Madame Celina,' they touch their helmets before turning and walking into the diner.

CHAPTER 7

*O*nce we have left the diner, we climb back onto Bob and continue in silence for a while until, eventually, my curiosity gets the better of me.

'Those two guards back there, they seemed like they knew you,' I say, attempting to make it sound like a casual observation.

'One of them did,' Celina replied.

'How?'

'What do you mean, how? What's with all the questions?' She responds in annoyance.

'I don't know. Maybe I'm curious because I'm literally putting my life in your hands. You say that I need to trust you, but I don't know you. I don't know who you are or whose side you're on. I don't even know what your intentions are toward me. That Gen Corp security guard back there knew you better than I do. What if you just want to sell me yourself, or keep me as your slave, huh? We haven't even been introduced,' fidgeting to get off the horse. She puts her arm across my chest, holding me in place.

'What are you doing? Are you trying to fall off?'

'No, I'm trying to get off.'

'You're gonna fall and trust me, it's a long way down and it hurts.' Bob neighs loudly, as if to agree with her.

'Look, my name is Celina alright, and I am not going to sell you! Now can you please stop struggling?'

'Hello, I am Adam,' I respond raising a brow at my sarcastic tone.

'Damn how did a moody thing like you survive the Adam program?' She chuckles.

'It wasn't hard no one annoyed me like you do,' I shoot back.

'Really' she drawls still amused. 'Is that really your name because you know that's what you are,' she states, and it really annoys me.

'Like I have never literally realised that until now,' I snap.

'No need to be rude,' she huffs.

'Sorry not having a name is annoying but also clever okay,' I glare at her. Sagging as all the fight leaves me. 'Please, just let me go, I'll be fine, no one need know we even met okay.' My face flushes with blood from the stress as my eyes fill with tears at the overwhelming urge to just let go and, well, just give in to the uncertainty and the inadequate way she makes me feel. I hadn't planned for this, for her. 'Please,' it comes out in defeat. That one word, with its pathetic inflection, sums me up.

'They would know, they always know, and you wouldn't last two minutes out here,' she says from behind me as she slowly relaxes her hold on my chest. Her voice is soft, not quite gentle, but it has lost its brash nature.

'Who would know? Who are they, Gen-Corp? What aren't you telling?' I demand anger getting the better of me.

'You don't know do you, Gen-Corp hah, you would be better off if they found you there are worse out here and you,' she shakes her head. Well, that deteriorated quickly. We are back to shouting.

'Please, my life is short anyway, don't make it shorter,' I plead, taking her hand in mine. It is the same size as mine, in fact, we are a similar build. I squeeze her hand, feeling the rough skin where she holds Bob's reins. 'Just let me go. If I die, it will be on my terms,' I am begging now.

'Listen, you muppet, I know all about what happens to Adams. I work for the United Human Federation. I'm here to help you,' she says. I am silent for a moment, trying to take in what she has said.

'The what?'

'The United Human Federation, surely you have heard of us? We rescue Adams and transport them to the independent territories.' She continues pulling back on Bob's reins and bringing him to a stop.

'I can't believe you hadn't figured it out,' she finishes climbing down and looking up at me with indignation.

'Figured what out? I've never even heard of the United Human Federation. How do I know you're not just making this all up?' I ask, suddenly feeling powerful from my lofty position on the horse.

'Well, if you stop trying to run away, I'll prove it to you,' Celina places her hands on her hips. Even from where she is, down on the ground, her entire posture and expression is one of superiority.

'Fine, I'll come with you, but I still don't fully trust you.' I climb gracelessly down from Bob and stand face to face with her.

She scowls before cracking a smile. 'Good, now get back on the horse.'

She turns off the road into a small wood that has grown up around the ruins of the buildings that used to be the outskirts of the town. She jumps down and doing the same; I follow her as she leads the horse deeper into the wood until she finds a small clearing that is relatively free from snow. Three sides have the ruined walls of long-ago abandoned building shielding us from the bitter wind.

Celina unties the tent from Bob and carefully unpacks it. Taking a quick glance at the instructions and then throwing them down, she ignores them. She stalks around with various bits of tent in her hands. Standing with Bob, I watch as the tent takes shape, trying not to laugh when she curses.

'Why can't we stay at that inn we saw back on the road?' My voice is truculent, and I am so past caring I don't even try to hide it. I'm not at all convinced by the tent; it looks flimsy and uncomfortable. Camping is definitely not my thing.

When I last went camping with Mathew and a couple of the other boys, I seem to recall we ate a lot of junk food until we felt sick, all while trying to ignore the fact that sleeping on the ground is uncomfortable.

'Because Adam...., is that really your name?'

'Yes,' I grumble.

'Odd, anyway, firstly it looked grimy as all hell and secondly it's too dangerous,' she answers, gazing at me evenly before going back to what she is doing.

'You have movement papers for me, so what is the problem?'

'The problem is they aren't yours and it won't be too hard for anyone to realise that, if they are able to get a proper look at them.' She turns her back on me as I frown.

'If those papers weren't for me, then you weren't at the cave looking for me. So why were you there? Who are those papers really for?'

'That, Adam, is none of your business,' she snaps, not even bothering to look at me. I bite my lip, suddenly filled with doubt about her intentions.

'You gonna stand there all day?' She asks, popping her head back out of the tent.

'Yeah, what's it to you?'

'Whatever, useless brat!' not sure I was meant to hear that, but a wide grin splits my face. My indecision shelved. She, it would seem is my best chance at freedom.

She collects the rest of the things we brought and her bags. She leaves the tent to sort out Bob. Once inside, I am quite impressed at the size of the tent. At the back, there is a zipped-up flap where Celina put the sleeping bags. The front part is an awning with mock windows in the plastic front bit. On the floor lay two fold up chairs, folded table along with a camping stove. Arranging the chairs first, I pick up the small camping stove, frowning as I read the instructions before putting it together and gingerly lighting it, visions of nuclear type explosions filtering through my brain, along with visions of burning to death.

She smiles when she comes in. Indecision swamps me despite what she told me earlier. Could I take her in a fight if it came to it? Who am I kidding? I bet she has been combat trained, whereas I certainly have little to no experience with fighting. I chew my thumb nail while I watch her. The most burning question in me, who do those papers belong to?

She rummages in the bags and pulls out an assortment of winter clothes. She has the same, except her jumper is red and mine is blue.

'Thanks.' I shuffle out of my damp clothes, which aren't easy in the confines of the tent. There is no stopping the shivers in just my boxers despite the warmth the burner is creating. Pulling the trousers on, I see Celina has stripped. I have never seen a semi-naked girl before. Mentally slapping myself, as I try valiantly to control my stupid body, I feel a blush heating my cheeks as I turn away from her.

'What's the matter, Adam?' She gazes at me, one eyebrow

raised as she surveys my body. Trust me, if Gen-Corp turned up now, I would go with them rather than suffer this.

'N... Nothing!' My hands shake, fumbling with the buttons on my shirt. She smirks at me, and I am sure she knows exactly what is making me so uncomfortable. I think I hate her in that moment. As she turns away and pulls on her trousers, her bottom brushes against me. Was it deliberate? To annoy me even more. Her way of punishing me for earlier, when I had been annoying her with all my questions?

Would she be that petty? As if things couldn't get worse, my traitorous body reacts. I haven't been milked in days. Don't get me wrong, I do not want that, but my body has expectations, is trained to react in certain ways to certain stimuli. How the hell am I supposed to pretend I am in control? Closing my eyes, I let out a sigh. She is just a girl. You have read about them; they aren't so different to you. When I open my eyes, she stands directly in front of me.

'Here, let me do that,' she reaches for my shirt, stepping closer. Her fingers brush my skin as I swallow. With nimble dexterity, she fastens all the buttons except the top two on my shirt.

'There you go,' she smiles before turning away to tidy up the discarded clothing.

'Thank you... for helping me.' She casts a look at me. Our eyes meet, and she turns away.

'Just a shirt, no big deal,' she mutters while folding my damp jeans the one's she lent me.

'No not that...' my voice trails off.

'Save it, I haven't yet,' she mutters, so quietly that I wonder if I was supposed to hear her. She lifts the pan off the burner and pours the hot water into two mugs. Putting the pan down, she reaches into her bag and produces two little containers. 'Do you want milk and sugar in your tea?'

'Yes please, what did you mean, you haven't yet?' I sip the

tea. It tastes awful from the powdered milk, but I don't care, it is hot and fills my stomach; I am impressed that she is so organised.

'Exactly what I said!' She doesn't look at me as she turns the burner off, placing it outside. Damn, I glance at her, taking in her appearance, from her scuffed boots to her bitten nails. You stupid idiot, Adam, you are worth a fortune. Her ticket to the good life.

'Are you going to exchange me for him?' Really didn't want to ask but felt compelled. I wait silently, swallowing some hot tea, which immediately makes my eyes water and my throat burn.

'I don't know yet!' She turns and looks at me, studying my face.

'Oh well, when you decide. Don't forget to inform me.'

'And there it is again,' she laughs, looking at me as if seeing me for the first time.

'What? This is me okay. Why I ran. I don't want to be someone's toy. I want to be me not spend my time pleasing someone else, okay,' I turn away from her annoyed.

'The thing is my boy was a retiree. You are underage, a runaway and technically, as per the agreement with Gen-Corp, I should give you back.' I turn back to her. Would she give me back? No, she said it doesn't work like that.

'When you say you, you mean the United Human Federation?'

'Yes.'

'They have treaties with Gen-Corp?'

'Yes, of course they do!'

'So, you have been matched.'

'What, yes,' she frowns at me, oh I am annoying her again. I seem to be good at that.

'Where is he?'

'Gen-Corp still has him. Hopefully, he is okay and once I

meet up with the others, we can open a dialogue with them and re-arrange the exchange.' Her expression hardens as she gets up. 'I am going to sleep.' I watch her shuffle into the other part of the tent. Alone, I sit and think about what she said.

CHAPTER 8

We spend the morning galloping through the deserted, and from what I could tell, abandoned countryside.

'Where are the people?' I ask, having grown bored with clopping along in silence.

'Oh um, most of them moved to the cities after the extinction and civil unrest... for safety, you know,' she answers absently, concentrating on the path in the snow.

'Was it terrible? I mean, they let us read bits but obviously they paint a slightly more optimistic picture.'

'Yeah, it was bad. As the male population dwindled along with the birth rate, governments had to decide which bits of the infrastructure to keep going, do they keep power stations running, television networks, telephone networks that sort of thing. With not enough work force, they forced people into different jobs, prioritising what was important. Schools closed as there were no children to go to them.'

'How did Gen-Corp get control, governments must of resisted?'

'No, not really. Governments had no clue what to do and,

as food ran out, the riots started. Gen-Corp was like this shining white knight. They had a plan and the workforce to implement it. By the time most governments realised it was too late, Gen-Corp owned the planet. With the Adam program promising a future, governments either fell into line or were eliminated.'

'Ireland did. They even resisted the contraceptive and rejected the Adam program.'

'Yes, Ireland did, but even though they didn't have the contraceptive, it was still too late, as it was in everything, so they lost their men and fertility like everywhere else, just not as fast,'

'Is that where you are from? I noticed your accent.'

'Yes.'

'Is that where you will take me?'

'Yes, eventually, you will be safe there.'

'Yes, I read about Ireland. I was going to go there once I found my brother.' Did I want to tell her that?

'You have a brother?' I nod but impart no more information.

'Where are we going now?' She speeds up again as I cling to her. From the way the horse reacts, I feel he is enjoying this. Unlike me, I feel like every joint I possess is being jolted with each of his steps. Eventually we stop and I climb down, stretching my limbs. Celina does the same, leading Bob behind us. I wait patiently for her to answer my question.

'Somewhere safe so I can plan our next move.' She answers at last, and it isn't the answer I want. It is her usual ambiguous answer.

'I don't need you to plan my next move. I know where I am going, thank you.'

'Whatever your plan was, it has changed now; you are with me.' I pick up on the annoyance in her voice.

'No, I am not with you, this isn't a permanent arrangement, just so we are clear on this', I feel her tense, guess she didn't like my tone.

'Adam, do you have any idea what could happen to you out here?'

'Yes, I could die, but since that was my fate anyway, it really isn't much of a gamble.'

'So, you know what happens to Adam's then?'

'Yes, I know what happens to Adam's. I'm also fully aware of the dangers I face out here, but there is someone I must find and in order to do that I need to get to Glasgow.'

'Your brother,' I nod again. 'Glasgow, you know Scotland isn't controlled by Gen-Corp,' she glances over her shoulder.

'No, I didn't. Who controls it?'

'No one, not really. It is lawless. Various clans rose and divided it. You can't go there. It is very dangerous, if they caught you... they have an illegal slave trade, illegal Adams taken used to breed. We have rescued a few and I am telling you it would of be kinder to euthanise those boys,' her voice is angry.

'I must go. I have to know. Why move him there if he wasn't going to be safe. I have to start somewhere.'

'So, you don't think he is still there then?'

'He might be, but it is unlikely, I need to check the record office.'

'What if you come with me now and I help you find him? We have access to all the databases; I could look for you.'

'Why would you do that?'

'Let's just say my life isn't that much better than yours, admittedly I won't be killed. Well, I hope not, but certain things are expected of me now I am matched. Also, there is a strong chance you are going to get sick.' Her voice softer, the annoyance gone.

'What, why?'

'We have shut you away, you haven't been exposed to the

levels of contaminant that you will out here, and it will make you sick. In the home, they would have implemented measures to limit your exposer to the contaminant. As it broke down, it became toxic. Out here the people well they have a certain immunity, but you won't. We have been dealing with this problem with the Adams for several years now,'

'How sick,' this isn't something I considered, and I am worried how sick I will get! I have never come across this information while researching the contraceptive. Gen corp isn't likely to let it be known that once you have bought your Adam he will probably die. I can't help smiling at the irony of that.

'That, I don't know everyone reacts differently.'

'Well, that sucks,' turning away so she can't see the obvious dismay on my face. Will I die? I question myself? Damn it, why does everything have to end in me dying?

'Adam, it will be fine I promise,' she is behind me, her hand is on my shoulder. The urge to brush it off is overwhelming, but I know that would upset her again.

'Yeah, sure,' I shrug, turning toward her while marshalling my features to hide the fear and uncertainty.

'Come on we need to find somewhere to spend the night,' she tries to make her tone upbeat but, well it isn't working.

CHAPTER 9

Leaning against the tree, I munch on the muesli bar. It is, I decide a lot like eating bird seed. Well, how I imagine eating bird seed would be. As I haven't eaten bird seed, but that's probably beside the point. I look up from my muesli; we are in a small clearing in a wood. Pine and fir trees all around me, silent witnesses to our rest stop.

'Here,' Celina hands me a cup of tea.

'Where are we going?' Pushing away from the tree, I walk to where Bob waits patiently.

'There is a UHF safe house nearby. Hopefully, there will be back up there so we can get you safely out of the country,' she answers, looking at something on her phone. It's one of those smart phones. We weren't allowed them at the boy's home and I would like a proper look at it just out of curiosity; apparently, they can do many things besides phoning people. Gen Corp kept that, communication they deemed important. I suspect phones are prohibiting expensive. A bit like Adams I muse.

'Safety where though?' One time, I would like her to just

give me a straight answer. She isn't listening. She is taking the tent down. I tip the last of my tea away.

'Right, let's get going,' she declares, getting to her feet and folding up her sleeping bag. I do the same. She wastes no time packing away the tent and the rest of our belongings. I stand to one side as she efficiently gets the tent in its bag. I struggled just getting my sleeping bag in its bag! Celina frowns at me, as I still seem to get in her way and annoy her. She loads it all onto Bob, who is currently grazing and paying us no attention.

She then turns her attention to me, zipping my coat right up and pulling the hood up. She tidies my hair, which she tucks away into the hood. Pulling the toggles tight, I try not to flinch at her touch, but do. She smiles at me, and I look anywhere but at her face. I am embarrassed that she is trying to help me and yet I still flinch at her touch.

'Adam, look at me,' Celina commands. I lift my head at the order; I am programmed to obey any female voice. How annoying is that?

'Where we are going now will be very dangerous. You must do as I say, no matter how stupid it might sound, do you understand! Do you trust me?' She searches my face, her green gaze intent.

'Yes,' and it is the truth. I trust her with my life, which I feel has already been demonstrated.

'If something happens to me, you make your way here,' she shoves a folded piece of paper into my hand. 'You go there do you understand tell them I sent you. What you don't do is try to help me. Do you understand? You don't help me, you run.' She repeats.

'Yes,' I manage, as the paralysing fear I have been trying to suppress surges through me again. I slept little last night, thinking about finding Aaron and leaving the home, stuff crashing about in my head. I woke wrapped around her. In my sleeping bag but still it was embarrassing and awkward. We travel in silence. I am still utterly fascinated by the country side and the abandoned villages we pass through. My imagination contouring up images of how I think it might have been. I am desperate to draw some of it but know Celina would never allow that. She is in an odd mood. We are both tired, so I keep my question to myself today.

'I don't need you to protect me,' her voice interrupts my daydreaming.

'I am well aware of that,' I scoff. 'Why would you think such a thing?'

'You talk in your sleep, Adam,' she sniggers at me as I feel the furious blush on my face.

'Better than snoring,'

'I do not snore,' her indignation comical as I chuckle.

'Yeah you tell yourself that,' The movement of Bob eventually lulls me to sleep.

'Where are we going?' I ask, blinking sleep out of my eyes, leaning against Celina. She smiles at me. I feel comfortable as Celina has her arm around me, holding me against her front. She lets go so I can sit up straighter.

'My place, and then the safe house,' she answers, concentrating. The snow has made everything the same level, and it is hard to see the road. Celina doesn't want Bob to fall in a ditch or something.

'You have a place?' I ask, and realise almost straight away I have upset Celina, as she stiffens against me.

'Well, yeah, I don't normally sleep in barns and tents,' Celina snaps back at me.

'Sorry, I meant I thought you lived with your group the human thingy,' I explain, taken aback by her defensive answer.

'Sorry Adam, that was rude,' Celina mumbles.

'It's okay you must be tired,' using a soothing tone I feel her relax.

'I use this place when I have a mission; I live with my mum or the colony otherwise. Sorry I snapped at you.'

'It's okay,' I lapse into silence. 'Why is your place so dangerous?' I ask, frowning, trying to join all the conversations together. 'If it is, why go there?'

'Because I don't want you sleeping in the tent more than you have to. When you get sick, I want you safe in a house. I don't know how bad your reaction will be.' Well damn, that wasn't the answer I was expecting.

Celina takes the long route into the city, keeping to the least used streets. Not that many people are about in this weather, but it can't hurt to be cautious. I take in our surroundings. I have never been to the city, obviously. I have only seen pictures in books, and they are nothing like this. This is dirty and run down, it just screams abandonment and I huddle into Celina, while utterly fascinated by it.

The buildings are crumbling like half eaten cake. Some have weed shrubs growing through them and I suppose nature will reclaim them completely eventually. The road is full of potholes and has grass growing through the tarmac. The tips of the grass pokes through the snow. Someone has cleared a path through the snow on this road so I guess it must be used. Not that we have seen anyone. Do I want to see anyone? All the things Celina has said makes me believe people are dangerous. Still, they fascinate me with there existence.

The poverty slowly gives way to commercial premises, which gives way to tree-lined avenues, with large houses that, although tired looking, are tidy. Even the snow has been shovelled into tidy piles.

'Celina, where are the people?' My question bubbled up as my gaze drank in the houses.

'Inside.' Well that wasn't much of an answer I knew that already.

'What do you mean inside?' Annoyance laced my voice and there was no way I could hide it. She stiffens as she draws in a breath. I know I am trying her patience, but I need this information for when I leave her.

'Adam, the city is very dangerous for everyone, not just you,' Celina answers distractedly as she concentrates on our route.

'Why?'

'Why, what?' Her voice terse and I smile, so I am annoying her again. I know I shouldn't find amusement in that, but I do.

'Stop grinning like that,' Celina growls and my grin gets wider.

'Why is it dangerous for everyone, not just us?' composing my features so I look serious.

'Because there are rules, laws and curfews, vermin sweeps, that have to be obeyed, especially here in Madame Trent's territory.'

'What's vermin sweep? Are there lots of rats?' Celina, laughing is not the reaction I expect and yes, I feel offended.

'No, Adam, there aren't rats, well not furry ones anyway.'

'Oh,' I don't understand, but she thinks I am stupid as it is, so I ask no more questions. 'Can I walk for a bit?' I ask instead. My legs ache sat on Bob for hours at a time.

'Yeah, sure,' she pulls Bob to a stop and we both slide off his back. We walk in silence; Bob follows behind us. I glance at Celina and then trail my hand along a wall, picking up a handful of snow, crushing it between my fingers.

Celina takes in a breath and rubs her face. I can see she is thinking. She bites her lip and gazes at me. I play with the snow while trying to avoid her gaze, wondering what she is about to say.

'Adam, have you ever read George Orwell's Animal farm?' She holds my gaze, and I am really confused. How is this relevant?

'Um, yes, I studied it for English. How is that relevant?' I frown. I really don't understand her line of questioning. Then again don't know why I studied it for English or why I had to learn all that stuff when all I am required to do in this world is make babies.

'Well, you see that is sort of what happened when the men died, and yes I know that book is referring to communism but that sort of happened as well,' Celina sighs her shoulders slump, and she looks tired.

'Yeah, I know but what does that have to do with me? As far as I know being sold to a stranger to have sex wasn't part of the communist ideal,'

'Wasn't it? Isn't it all in the interpretation?'

'What? No.' She is seriously annoying me now.

'You know my fate is no different to yours,' I raise a brow at that statement.

'Really you have been locked away. Knowing you will either be sold or killed on your twentieth birthday. Gosh I never knew,' my voice drips with sarcasm. She has the grace to blush.

'Sorry,' she mutters. I feel bad now. I don't want to feel bad. She is not my friend. I remind myself.

'Celina, will you just get to the point?' I growl, frustrated by her stupid questions and answers.

'Okay, mister moody, the thing is the Madams are the pigs stepping into the role of the men or humans and do you remember the puppies in the book?' I nod.

'Yeah, the pigs take them and educate them, and they become the pig's security.' I answer, still not sure where this is going.

'Well, the Madams have their own version, who do as

they say, without question, they roam the suburbs of the town and if they catch us...' her voice trails off.

'I get it we die,' I say, looking at Celina directly.

'Not necessarily for you, anyway. There are worse things than dying,' she whispers.

'What does that mean?' I demand, and I know that came out harsh, but what the...

'It is common knowledge Madame Trent—well, she is well known for her brutality. We have already confiscated an Adam from her and let's just say—he didn't adjust well,' she looks me over. 'You are so beautiful,' she reaches and brushes my hair from my face, and I let her. Her touch so soft as she bites her bottom lip our gaze lock. 'If she saw you well... let's just say it won't end well,' she steps back, the spell broken.

'I see, so you think it is safer to go through, that I am weak and going around is too risky,' I finish. I know, that was blunt, but well, it had to be said.

'That burger restaurant we visited the other day was in the middle of the sticks. You saw how busy it was, the number of Gen-Corp troopers that were eating there. The suburbs are lawless, just like the countryside, but way more people live there. Gen-Corp security patrols them all the time just to keep the gangs in check. I don't want you to get caught up in firefight or routine vermin sweep.'

'Okay, how does that make sense if Gen-Corp controls the inner cities? Surely there is even more chance of us getting caught there?' I reply, unconvinced by Celina's strategy.

'Maybe the chance of getting caught is slightly higher, but the actual physical danger we would be in is much lower. Besides, as the inner city is secure, there will be way fewer security guards to worry about.'

'That still makes little sense to me, but if you think it's

safer, then I guess that is what we'll do,' I reply, running my hand through my hair, while puffing out my cheeks.

'I... um, yes, but what I didn't add was there are the common people to consider as well.' Celina adds, and I frown. The common people? Are we still doing Animal Farm metaphors, or does she mean what she is saying? I sigh, shoving my hands in my pockets, as I don't know what to do with them.

'You look so cute when you do that,' Celina mutters. I glare at her. Is now really the time?

'Celina, concentrate, please,' I say, my cheeks reddening.

'Sorry, it's just your perfectness is distracting,' Celina says looking away.

'Perfectness is that even a word!' I exclaim. I can't believe we are having this conversation.

'Sorry,' Celina's mouth turns up in a lopsided smirk; I can't help it. I grin back.

'You were telling me about common people?' I prompt trying to get this conversation back on track.

'Oh yeah, sorry, well the thing is there is discontent, and most people are poor, really poor and dissatisfied, if they got hold of you, well, I don't know, you are valuable, really valuable,' Celina's shrug is nonchalant, but I am sure that is her way of making it trivial. When we both know it isn't.

'Oh,' is all I can manage.

'So, are you sure this is what you want? It isn't too late to go back?' She cocks her head to one side as if she is assessing me. She does this a lot, and I find it endearing. 'I can contact Gen-Corp and have them collect you,' It takes a while for her last sentence to register but when it does, I almost explode.

'What, are you mad? Do you have any idea how hard it was to escape? I want to see things, do stuff not be shut away and then retired, sold, whatever happens to old Adams.' I run my hand through my hair, aware I haven't explained that very well. She is laughing at me again.

'Oh, pack it in!' I glare at her, although I quite like that she thinks I'm cute. I am getting attached to her and I mustn't. She isn't mine. Those papers she has aren't mine they are for another boy. Her genetic match. 'I need to find my brother, see him once more,' I whisper. I mustn't get distracted by this quirky funny girl who I suspect has already wormed her way into my heart. My mind conjures up a cartoon heart with a cute worm living in it. Good grief Adam you are losing it mate my inner voice mocks.

'I know, I do understand,' her smile is brief as a sadness seems to settle over her. We clamber back onto Bob.

CHAPTER 10

Celina takes Bob to a stable that appears to be communal. I admire the architecture. The large wooden doors with their oval top that fits into the oval stonework. The grey stone with its large blocks is impressive. Out where I am stood is cobbles with a central drain. This place bustles with activity with the overwhelming smell of horses.

Concealed behind a wooden post. I watch Celina as she talks to a woman in an office type room. The pleasure I feel at seeing something intact is ridiculous. It is such a contrast to the devastation we have passed on the way here. The ruins of the buildings a disappointment. Not at all like the pictures in my books. Just skeletons of what had been. Bleach bones of human habitation.

Turning it annoys me that Celina has just left me, spying Bob's back end disappear into what I assume is his horse box. Huffing, I make my way in that direction.

'You're a boy?' A hand on my arm drags me to a stop. I glance at the figure to my side.

'So, what if I am.' I raise a brow and give her my most imperious glare.

'I might just take you,' a knife, cold at my throat. I blink while working out my options.

'Oh, really and you think I would just go along with that?' She is a slight little thing and for once I believe I could take her. Oh, the irony my sarcastic thought.

'Yes,' her breath against my neck had goose bumps erupt over my skin. 'You are exquisite, such beauty is wasted on The United Human Federation.' She is pressed against my back her knife still at my throat. Boldly I reach up and push it away with little resistance.

'If that's the case, what are you offering,' my voice has a seductive quality to it making her smile.

'Oh, you are trained well I like that,' her voice in my ear as her tongue licks my neck. I shudder at the intimacy of it.

'Anna, leave him alone,' Celina's voice breaks the spell and the girl steps away from me.

'Celina, you should take better care of your toys,' the girl Anna mocks still looking me over. 'I can give you a life of privilege and wealth, a beautiful specimen like you would have your pick of ladies to pleasure with me as your Madame.' She glances over at Celina while running her hand down my body. She moves around me. She has a feline agility to her.

'You would let another take me, teach me?' I hold her gaze as she stops moving. Behind me again I can feel her pressed against me her breath ruffles my hair as she whispers in my ear.

'Oh no, I would make it my personnel business to train you,' her hand trails down as her other hand moves my head and her lips brush mine. Stepping away she chuckles. 'You would enjoy that wouldn't you,' a smirk dances over her lips.

'He is underage Anna,' Celina frowns as she pulls me away clearly agitated.

'Oh, I enjoy them young. Easier to train no bad habits.' She winks at me.

'Oh, I don't have time for this,' Celina sighs pulling me after her.

'Thanks,'

'For what?' Her green-eyed gaze is intense as she finally looks at me.

'I don't know finding me, leaving me out there, saving me,' I gesture toward the street. 'If you hadn't done the first two the third one wouldn't have occurred,' I grumble with annoyance.

'Oh, whatever,' she puts hay in a rack.

'Mature,' it leaves my mouth before I can stop it.

'You are such a girl I don't know why I am hiding you,' her green eyes rake over me once more, before she puts the saddle and bridle on a rack.

'Yeah whatever,' it is my nerves making me behave this way, shoving my hands in my pockets to stop them from shaking. I am tired and emotional in this new and strange place where danger lurks around every corner ready to devour me. This was what I wanted wasn't it? An adventure to see the world, well what's left of it. Somehow, I realise it isn't matching up to my expectations. This thought annoys me.

Returning my attention to the girl she is looking at me in that way she has. Sort of worried but sorry and sympathetic all at the same time and it annoys me– a lot. Her touch is soft and gentle despite the calloses on her palms where she rides Bob. She touches me a lot recently almost as if she needs reassurance that I truly exist. How long have I been letting her invade my space? Why haven't I put a stop to this intimacy? Because you like it my inner voice points out.

'Adam?' She pulls my hands from my pockets. Seeing them shake, she holds them. 'Okay,' her eyes hold mine. That one word seems to crash through a barrier tearing it to shreds and stomping all over it. As she builds her house in my heart and I can't stop her, or I don't want to stop her. I can't decide which.

'Okay,' it comes out in a whisper. Her face lights up with a smile as a tentative one pulls at my lips. Terrified is the overriding feeling smothering me now. My stomach seems to tie itself in knots and it is all I can do not to throw up. Celina takes my hand, and we walk out of the stables; she stops and looks at me.

'I am sorry about Anna she was always bold,'

I shrug, 'It's alright I knew you wouldn't let her take me,' Celina takes me outside her hand firmly wrapped around mine.

'We need to run. You don't stop for anything, do you understand? We are heading for 54 Corner Road. You go there and find Madame Betty, she will keep you safe, okay,' Celina searches my face and I swallow. I nod, unable to speak, shoving my hands in my pockets as fear makes them shake. Celina adjusts the strap of my bag. Her hands sort of linger on me. I notice she is nervous and realise she wasn't trying to scare me earlier; this really is as dangerous as she says.

'Ready!' I just nod, unable to speak.

We dash through the streets. The houses and shops pass in a blur as I concentrate on keeping up with Celina. I hear shouting and gunfire. Celina's hand tightens on mine as she pulls me along. She runs up some steps to a town house that looks like it has seen better days. All the paintwork is now tired. Celina rummages in her pocket and, producing a key, she slides it into the lock, pushing the door open. Grabbing me, she shoves me inside with such force I almost fall. Shutting the door firmly behind us, we both lean over for a minute, getting our breath back after the run. Celina turns to me and pushes the hood of my coat down so she can look at me, searching my face again.

'Are you okay, Adam?' Her voice, conveying her concern for me.

'Yes, I'm fine; I am capable of running, you know.' I answer crossly. She treats me like some delicate child sometimes, like I might break at any minute, and it is annoying me. I stiffen when a voice sounds from somewhere in the house, a shaft of light illuminating the hallway from a door opening.

'Celina, girl, where you been? You said you were going for chips and then there was that murder, and I was worried for you, you been gone for days. What was I going to tell your poor mother?' A large, round woman appears in the hall from the lit-up doorway. She glares at both of us. Her gaze lingers on me as she takes in every detail. She must be able to see I am a boy, yet no shock registers on her round, lined face. This makes me assume she is Madame Betty.

'I got asked to run an errand, and then I got caught in that blizzard, and I found this poor soul, so we took shelter until it passed.' Celina explains, giving Madame Betty her best vulnerable look. I am impressed as I can see Madame Betty melting, as she gazes at us both, before she huffs, folding her arms under her very ample bosoms.

'Well, you both look frozen. Better get in my kitchen so I can warm you both up. Madame Betty smiles at us and we shuffle into Madame Betties' flat. The flat is decorated in loud colours; it smells of cinnamon and furniture polish along with some other scents that I can't identify. It is, I decide, a nice homey smell. The furniture, although old, is well looked after and the addition of colourful rugs and cushions just add to the safe, comfortable atmosphere. I feel myself relax.

The warmth wraps around us both, making me feel my face heat as I glance at Celina, I see she has red cheeks and guess mine must be the same, the smell of something cooking makes both our stomachs rumble as we pull out chairs and sit down at the well-scrubbed pine table.

'So, who is your friend?' Madame Betty asks, ladling hot stew into two bowls and passing them to me and Celina. She then cuts generous slices of bread, buttering each piece, placing them on a plate between us. I slip my coat off and hang it on the back of my chair.

'Um, Amy,' I mumble around mouthfuls of stew. It was the first name I could think of. The stew is delicious, and I am feeling warm again. Madame Betty glares at me but makes no comment about my answer. A small smile dances around her mouth, as her gaze returns to Celina.

I know she doesn't believe me, and I know I should worry about that fact. The hunger that has been competing with the cold for my attention has finally gone away. I focus on the conversation Celina and Madame Betty are having.

'Celina, darling, do I look stupid? Now where did you get this, Adam?' She glares at Celina. I swallow, frightened. This could go horribly wrong. Celina just smiles, a slow smile, her eyes lighting up with mischief.

'Aw, come on Madame Betty, you know me, it was chance.' Madame Betty looks at her and sighs with exasperation.

'Oh, come on then, let's hear it.' Madame Betty sits down, a resigned expression on her face. I look at them both, waiting for Celina to speak, enjoying how relaxed they are with each other. I am growing to like Celina. Of course, now I know she isn't going to kill me, sell me, or try to have sex with me. I am a bit more relaxed around her.

'Well, I was going for chips. Oh, Adam, have you ever had chips from a chip shop? No, of course you haven't.' She answers her question before I can, so I shake my head. Well, I have had chips, but I strongly suspect they are nothing like the chips Celina is talking about. I have certainly never been to a chip shop. I would like to though, it sounds amazing.

'Really, well, I will get you some while we are here,' Celina replies. She is so animated it makes me smile.

'Celina, dear, what happened when you went for chips?' Madame Betty prompts.

'Well, you know, I got a call from Thom,' Celina looks at Madame Betty for longer than I thought was polite. Thom? Who is this Thom? Are they female? Before I can ask Madame Betty climbs to her feet.

'Bedtime I think,' Madame Betty announces. Shuffling to the door we dutifully follow. She shows us to her guest room. I gaze around, taking in the dark polished wood chest of drawers that match the large double bed, dominating the room with its bright knitted throw that contrasts against the white sheets. The smell of furniture polish reminds me of home. Home, was it home? No, not without Aaron. He was my home. I quickly strip down to my boxer's and climb into the enormous bed. I sigh at the softness of it and Celina laughs.

'You are so soft,' she scoffs.

'I am not; I just appreciate the finer things in life, like sleeping in a bed, not on the floor,' I reply with indignation, pulling the covers around me. Celina looks at me and then lets out a giggle. I like this version of Celina. Relaxed Celina is fun.

'Go to sleep Adam,' she steps out of the room and pulls the door too; I listen as she talks to Madame Betty.

'It was dangerous Celina. They didn't brief you. What if they had caught you?' Madame Betty replies, her voice full of concern. The Madame's know you. Why do you think they matched you to retire you,' Madame Betty huffs and I can imagine she has crossed her arms under her large bosom.

'I was going anyway. My boy was in that home, that's where I had been, with Thomas receiving the last details for my boy. I found him by accident; I couldn't get my boy, as the whole place was on lockdown. Emma saw me on the road and flagged me down, told me to go to the cave, that her boy would be there. She didn't tell me why, just to find him and keep him safe.'

'One of Emma's boys? What is he? He won't be a normal Adam if he is an Adam at all. All that pale hair and eyes. He isn't robust like a normal Adam. Does Thom know you have Emma's boy?'

'Yes, he knows, but he is tied up looking for those twins. What do you think he is? He is very small and delicate and an attitude that makes up for his diminutive frame. He is smart, questions everything. I have never seen such determination in an Adam.' It goes quiet before Celina speaks again. 'I lost my boy they still have him, and Gillian knows, she was there. That's why Emma was so flustered,'

'Hmm, Emma always trod a fine line when it came to ethics and Gillian knows that. Has he got sick yet? If he is one of Emma's he might not survive,'

'No, he hasn't, and I have considered that. He also knows that.'

'Oh Celina, I am so sorry about your boy. I know how much he meant to you. Celina, this is Madame Trent's territory, and it is common knowledge she has been after an Adam for a while, if she finds him...'

'I know, but he needs to be in a house with proper facilities, he is fragile. You know, it surprised me when he told me he was seventeen, I thought him younger. He would not cope with sleeping rough any longer. I had no choice but to come through the city. We feed him up, keep him hidden. You know he will get sick. I couldn't risk that out there. I will move him to the safe house as soon as I know it is safe to do so. I have informed Thom of my intentions and he agrees, we build the boy up and then move him.'

'Seventeen, I had him younger and I am pretty good at these things. He has to be from an experimental program if Emma is his Mother.' I hear feet shuffling and assume they are hugging. She knew I was in that cave. Mother sent her. Can I still trust her? Will she really help me find Aaron? What do they mean experimental? I am special but only because I am a twin, and they are rare.

Celina slips back into the room, and I pretend to be asleep. Wishing I hadn't heard that conversation and wonder who these people are, and if I am safe. Who was her boy? Did I know him? I feel Celina get into bed; she fidgets and gets comfortable. I listen as she falls asleep while I lay in the dark thinking about everything I have heard. She thinks I am pathetic, weak. I'm not I can be strong; I will show them, I think as I drift off to sleep.

CHAPTER 11

*S*itting in the garden as the sunshine warms my face, we have been here a couple of days and I am relaxing. I haven't seen Celina much in the day. She goes out early to see Bob and then somewhere else. I assume to do with her job, whatever that is exactly. The sickness Celina is so worried about hasn't occurred yet and I wonder if she made it up.

I have my drawing book and pencil case along with my map. I have marked where I am in relation to where Glasgow is, as I plan my next move. Aaron is still my priority, despite Celina's promises. I study and draw the snowy urban scene. I am so engrossed that I don't notice the little girl watching me from her perch on the fence.

'What yer doing?' she asks, glaring at me, making me startle and look up.

'Drawing.'

'Can I see?' She hops down before I can give her permission and saunters over to where I am sitting. She looks about seven or eight. I'm not very good a guessing age. After all, I look about fourteen, when I am seventeen, almost eighteen.

'Oh, that is my house!' She smiles, 'can you draw people?'

'Um, yes,' I turn the page and show her the pictures of Mathew and my Mother.

'Who are they?' She looks at me, intrigued, waiting for my answer.

'My Mother and my friend,' I answer, smiling at her.

'Do they live here with you? I live with my mum and aunty and cousin,' she reveals.

'No, they don't live here,' I mumble.

'Oh, can you draw me then, I promise to sit still,' she gazes at me, her eyes wide, in her grubby face, as she looks imploringly at me.

'Of course,' I smile, as she sits down and gets comfortable. She sits quietly for about two minutes, while I quickly draw her.

'Can I see it now?' she jumps up, rushing over to peer over my shoulder. 'Wow, that looks just like me!' She claps her hands together, hopping from one foot to the other, her excitement palpable. 'Can I keep it?' her gaze, a picture of hope.

'Yes, here.' I carefully tear it out and pass it to her.

'Thanks,' she gazes at it and then disappears over the fence. I am cold, so pack my things away to go inside and find Celina.

'Oh, Adam, you are freezing. Where have you been?'

'Outside, I was in the garden, um, drawing,' I feel silly telling her as heat steals up my cheeks.

'Did anyone see you?' she snaps.

'What, no, I mean yes, I um, drew a little girl. I was covered. She couldn't see,' I say tentatively, as I see Celina's expression change to one of anger.

'Adam, how stupid are you?' She hisses at me.

'I'm not stupid! I didn't know she was there until it was

too late. I just wanted to do something normal. Locked up in this house, I might as well be back in the home. Okay,' I am shouting at her, all the anger, frustration and fear pouring out. I look at Celina once more and then stalk down the hall to the bedroom, slamming the door behind me. I flop onto the bed and let the tears flow as I bury my face in the pillow.

'Adam, I'm sorry, Celina sits on the bed. She puts her hand on my shoulder and I don't mind. I turn over and sit up, pulling my legs up, so my chin rests on my knees, wrapping my arms around them.

'I'm sorry, Adam, I shouldn't have shouted, and I shouldn't have just left you here. When we get to Ireland, it will be different, I promise. We will even find you a match,' she smiles as I digest what she has said. The anger I feel rushes to the fore as I gape at her. I don't want any of that. Does she not know? That's why I ran to avoid being owned by some random woman.

'Well, ain't that great, I might as well of stayed where I was, thanks for rescuing me but next time don't bother,' I grind out my voice quivering with anger. 'Being dead kinda sounds appealing right now,' I retaliate.

'Don't be such an ungrateful git, we won't kill you at twenty,' Celina snaps.

'Well, you're assuming I live that long?' I snap back.

'Sorry,' Celina says quietly after all the shouting.

'Yeah, I'm sorry too,' I mutter, stunned by her outburst.

'Humanity is dying. We must do our duty,' Celina's voice is flat and emotionless. It annoys me and makes me so angry. Without thinking, I grab her and push her down, pinning her with my body. 'Duty, you want to do your duty. Here you go,' and I crash my lips to hers. Her eyes open in surprise as I kiss her. Until she pushes me off after all, it was only surprise that gave me the advantage.

'What the…. Adam,' she scrambles up with indignation.

'Welcome to my world,' I snarl out, turning my back to her wiping my mouth with the back of my hand. The room saturated in silence. I climb off the bed and back away from her. Grabbing up my things shoving them into my bag all the while shouting at her. 'You, you are no better than the people I have got away from. I am a person; I have feelings and aspirations.' I am so angry I am shaking as hot tears fall down my face. I didn't want to cry, so that just makes me angrier as I ball my hands into fists. 'I just want to find my brother. See him, you know, before we are both sold or euthanised. Why can't anyone understand that?' I reach for my coat pushing my feet into my boots at the same time getting ready to run.

Celina climbs off the bed and takes a tentative step toward me. 'You won't be forced into anything you don't want,' her hands up, trying to calm me. 'I said I would help you find him, didn't I. Please Adam don't run. I am sorry,'

'Yes, I know you did, but I can't trust you. Because all those things you said will happen to me if I stay with you. I wouldn't mind so much if I could do those things with you rather than a stranger, but I can't have you, can I?' I blurt, blushing when I realise what I have said.

'You would?' Celina asks as she stops in front of me, her eyes wide with surprise at my confession.

'Yes.' I gaze at my feet. I don't know what to do now. All these emotions crashing around inside me. My life was so ordered before and now I am in chaos most days. Don't get me wrong this is what I wanted the adventure. I just didn't factor in her and all these feelings washing through me. 'You are lovely, and kind and you know stuff. I have never met anyone like you before,' I give a mirthless chuckle. 'I haven't met anyone to be fair. So, I don't have anything to compare,' this comes out as a stutter much to my embarrassment. Her hands are on the strap to my bag. Lifting it over my head dropping it to the floor.

'Oh Adam,' she lifts my chin. 'I would like you to be mine as well, but I have a match,' she slips my coat off and it is very intimate having her undress me.

'I know,' kicking my shoes off as I slump onto the bed. I draw my legs up and hide my face behind my knees.

She kicks her slippers off and scoots up, so she is sitting next to me, pulling her legs up and wrapping her arms around them. We sit like that for a bit in silence.

'What was he like... your brother,' her gaze finds mine.

'He was, is fun and protective. He spent his time protecting me from them. From the world and our situation. People liked him and he them I suppose. I was the quiet one, hiding in his shadow,' I pull my sketch book out and flip the pages. Remembering his laugh and smell, the sound of his voice when he read to me. 'Here,' I pass her my book with the portrait I did of Aaron on our birthday. That was so long ago now. I suppose she knows what he looks like as we were identical, but this picture clearly shows another person. Not me. She turns some pages smiling at the pictures of Aaron.

'Who is this?' She stops at a picture of Mathew.

'That's Mathew. After Aaron went, he came and we immediately became friends even though he was older than me,' I smile as I think about Mathew. He will be with his match now. 'He was matched and leaving me... that's when I made up my mind to leave. I didn't want to be there anymore. It was run away or...find a way to end it all.' I look at her expecting to see disgust at my admission as she realises, I am a coward.

'No Adam don't say that.' The book is cast aside as she bundles me to her. 'Don't ever say that' her voice thick with emotion. 'Don't even think it my precious boy,' she mutters while peppering my face with kisses.

'Are you hungry?' Celina asks, her hands holding my face. I can see the glisten of tears. 'Why am I asking that? You're always hungry.' Her voice bright as she nudges me with her shoulder. The anger drains away as my body slumps against the bed headboard. Turning to look at her, a tentative smile pulls at my mouth.

'Yeah, you promised me chips from a chip shop.'

'Chips, it is then,' she kisses my cheek and scrambles off the bed.

'What is it with you and food wrapped in paper?' I ask, eyeing the paper parcels on the table. The most delicious smell is saturating the room. Celina laughs as she shares them out. I eat all of mine and half of Celina's.

'For someone so small, you eat a lot,' Celina chuckles, as I sit back, hardly able to move. I rub my stomach and grin.

'I have missed a lot of meals lately. I need to catch up.'

CHAPTER 12

Someone is shaking me. Turning over as Celina leans over me.

'Whoa Celina, what's going on?' Sitting up, rubbing my eyes. I frown at her. Still startled from her proximity.

'Adam, get dressed, someone must have seen us,' she throws my clothes at me as she shoves our stuff into the bag. I hurriedly get dressed and pull my boots on. I can hear shouting outside as I pull my coat on, doing up the zip. Following Celina, Madame Betty is nowhere to be seen. As Celina leads me out a side door, I hadn't noticed before.

'What's going on?' I try to keep the panic from my voice.

'When I went to get Bob this morning, the place was teaming with security searching the houses. They must be looking for us, sorry Adam,' she gazes into my eyes.

'Gen-Corp! well that's okay, isn't it?' My voice hesitant.

'Not Gen-Corp, local security,' She pulls me against a wall her whole being agitated.

'The Puppies,' I whisper as she nods her head.

'I am so sorry, I was meant to keep you safe,' her voice catches.

'It's not your fault,' I smile to reassure her, squashing the fear bubbling up inside me. We creep down a side alley. Celina stops and peers round a corner and slips into the next street. I am about to follow when I hear a shout.

'Oi, you, stop or we shoot,' I mouth "go" to Celina as I see her hesitate, slowly raising my hands above my head. I turn to face two securities pointing their guns at me. They march toward me as I swallow down my fear, pulling myself up to my full height, which isn't that intimidating, but it helps me feel confident.

'Adam, you will come with us.' they go to take my arms, but I move away, they lift their guns pointing at my chest.

'Don't touch me please, where is your Madame?' I try authority, watching various expressions cross their faces. I know just seeing me is a shock to them and I decide to use this to my advantage. I also know Celina will be somewhere hidden, watching and I need to buy her time. They lower their guns and look me over.

'I'm a registered Adam,' pushing my sleeve up to show them the number on my arm. They both look at it and then look at me.

'Move,' they both say together, pointing their guns at me again as they march me out of the alleyway and into the street.

I am marched to the front of the houses, noticing the Madame immediately as she gives orders. She turns in my direction. A fleeting smile crosses her face. I look her over arrogantly, and then arrange my features into a look of disdain.

She is tall and slim, dressed in a fitted business suit, her brown hair in an up do on the top of her head, giving her a severe look. She doesn't speak as she takes my arm and pushes the sleeve up, inspecting the number tattooed on my forearm. She drops my arm and I push my sleeve back down.

'Where is your Mother?' She asks, her voice cold and emotionless.

'I lost her,' I don't feel the need to say more than is necessary, as I inject arrogance into my voice. I am an Adam, and I know she knows there is a protocol she must follow regarding me and my return to Gen-Corp.

'Where have you been, and who has been helping you?'

'I have been living rough, while trying to make my way here.'

'Is that so?' She smiles at me again. A security officer walks over to the Madame, passing her a slip of paper, then turns and leaves. I try to see it, without success.

'I will need a sample.'

'Of course,' I answer curtly.

'But first I need you to see something,' she smiles coldly at me, and I am escorted back to the street where Madame Betties' house is. I swallow, I kinda know what is going to happen and my mind freezes, as I know it is my entire fault for being here, living amongst these people.

The entire street is teaming with security, as they herd all the people outside. They are lined up; the women gawp at me. I feel all colour drain from my face, my body turning cold as I search franticly for Celina and Madame Betty. I feel momentary relief at not seeing them.

It is only fleeting though, as I know what is going to happen. These innocent people are going to die because of me, and they don't even know me. Some teenagers spit at the guards as they go through, testing them and separating them out.

Removing the teenagers and women that are clean from their families and friends and dragging them away. To valuable a commodity to be wasted. Forced to become surrogates for the Adam program. The blood drains from my face as I know what will happen when this process is finished.

'No, please they didn't know,' I beg.

'Tell me who was helping you,' she looks at me as I stay silent. 'I thought as much,' her features twist with loathing. The security are lining the women up.

I watch as they do this in silence; the girls don't make a fuss or a sound. I shiver and remember the conversation I had with Celina when first coming here. How dangerous it is and all the rules. I am sure I am about to get a demonstration of the punishment for disobeying. Tears trickle down my face dripping onto the collar of my coat.

'Last chance Adam, who was helping you,' I shake my head in horror.

'No one ... no one was helping me please,' I beg.

The women are dressed as drab as the row of terrace houses, they currently stand in front of. The grey light filters through a break in the clouds as a soft drizzle covers everything in a fine mist. In a moment, I know they will paint the dirty cobbled street with their blood, and it will be all my fault. Part of me wants to join them. That death seems a relief of sorts. Easy, a brief pain before this struggle is over. My sick thoughts generate a kind of envy in me. I am truly a coward.

'I charge you with holding this Adam, the penalty for that is death,' the Madame shouts. The crowd goes quiet and a lone voice answer.

'We ain't had your poxy Adam. We are all virgins here, ain't we girls?' the voice is defiant and full of loathing, as a collection of nervous laughs echoes around the street. The Madame smiles and ignores the voice. Instead, she turns to me.

'This Adam, is what happens when you lie, do you understand?' she looks at me and as she does, she flicks her hand. The security open fire in one burst. They make no sound as they crumple to the ground. My anguished voice echoes around the buildings, blending with the staccato of the guns before the echo fades and silence reigns once more.

'No,' I shout, as two security guards take my arms and drag me away. My body twists as I struggle to get out of their grasp. A gust of wind blows the rain as a single sheet of paper floats lazily. A single punch to the gut stops my struggles.

'Search the houses, look for the girl with red hair. I want her found and if she isn't dead already, I want that corrected,' the Madame orders. She turns to me, and I glare at her through the tears.

'You thought I didn't know who was protecting you? The minute you entered my city I knew about you. These are my people this is my city and now you are mine. So, drop the arrogance you are mine now and Gen-Corp will not come looking.' She sneers at me, and I spit in her face. She wipes it off and then slaps me so hard I taste blood. 'I want that sample, Adam, and it would be better if you give it willingly,' she walks away from me, as I am dragged away.

CHAPTER 13

Marched down a corridor I try to see where I am. Stopping outside a door the guard unlocks it.

'Move,' the gun presses into my back as I am forced through the now open door. Inside is dark as I stumble forward. Turning as the door clangs shut. I lean against it my forehead absorbing the cold of the metal. My hands flat against it, as if I could will it open. Taking in deep breaths to push down the panic. I need a clear head if I am going to escape this.

Turning I peer through the gloom. A small rectangular window the only source of light. The bars across it pointless because frankly a rat couldn't squeeze through. I make out shapes huddled on the floor by the far wall. The odd sniffle coming from them. Blanking the sound out I concentrate on the room.

There is no furniture. Moving to the opposite wall to them and away from the door I sink down and bury my face in my drawn-up legs. A sigh leaves my lips at the futility of it all. Leaning back, I close my eyes. Exhaustion and despair fill me after the trauma of earlier. I can hear them shuffle about and breathing in the silence as I try to block it out. I don't want to have it made real by them being here. I know what and who they are.

'What will happen to us, Beth?' A timid voice breaks the silence. This immediately draws my attention.

'Shush Elle, it will be all right,' this voice is full of anger, and I open my eyes keeping my posture loose as if I am uninterested. The clean girls, young enough to breed. Breed with me. My hand slips into my bag where the knife is hidden. Luck was on my side when they didn't take my bag.

'No, it won't don't shield her from the truth,' a pale auburn-haired girl snarls with derision. She pushes to her feet and starts to pace. Stalking over to where I am huddled. Serendipitously I glance up at her keeping my posture loose as if I am asleep. She looks tired and with heavy bags under her eyes, which are red rimmed. Her limp hair slides forward.

'You girl! Why are you sat over here?' She squats down to get a closer look at me, her voice condescending. 'Well... would you look at that?' She sneers before standing and stepping away slightly. 'Stand Adam,' her voice commanding, and I must obey. Damn it.

'What are you doing Clara? Blazing blue eyes peer at me from a beautiful face framed by tightly braided hair decorated with beads her stance questioning. Moving to stand next to Clara, she appraises me. She sucks in a short breath as her eyes widen in shock.

'Is that an Adam?' She whispers and steps back. Fear leeks from her as she looks at me the embodiment of everything they fear most. There worst nightmare stood before them reminding them of the fate that awaits them if they can't escape this situation. A fear that is mirrored on my face.

'This, Adam... is the reason we are here. The reason our

families are dead.' Clara glares at me, her features cold. 'Come, get acquainted girls,' she sneers her bitter eyes refuse to shift from me. She pushes my hood down and undoes my coat. 'Let's have a look at you, since we are going to be so intimately acquainted,' Her hand is on my chest as I hold her gaze, she lets it travel downward. 'Are you good, obedient,' her voice callous as she whispers in my ear her hand now on my crotch. The knife from my bag is in my hand and pressed to her side.

'Do not touch me again,' I growl at her. Her arms drop to her sides as she frowns at me. Shock and surprise paint her features and my lips twist into a satisfied smile.

'Got a bit of bite,' she snaps her teeth together and I can't help but startle. She laughs and it is cold and bitter. Her hand slaps the knife from my grip. It clatters to the floor. Her gaze moves over me again her expression one of disdain. 'Pathetic,' her parting shot as she saunters away. My hands shake fumbling with the zip on my coat before sinking back down. Scrambling for the knife.

'Are you really an Adam?' A delicate creature that reminds me of a little bird shuffles over to me. Fine strawberry blond hair frames a round face. Large green eyes survey me as she bites her full bottom lip. She takes a timid step closer to me. Her features twisted in uncertainty. A curiosity born of fear.

'Yes, I am...,' my voice gentle so I don't frighten her. She kneels in front of me. Her eyes large in her face.

'Elle, what are you doing come here,' the auburn-haired girl hisses.

'I just want to talk to him, Beth,' Elle calls back still holding my gaze.

'Well, be quick, if the guards catch you,' Beth doesn't finish that sentence as Elle holds up her hand in a commanding be quiet gesture. Her attention still on me.

'Will it hurt… I heard it hurts… you know?... when…' she

wipes her face, dashing away the tears. 'I don't want to die. Not yet. I wanted to see the world a bit and do stuff.' her voice quiet and desolate. 'I wanted to fall in love,' she whispers.

'So did I,' my answer has her looking up at me. 'I won't hurt you and if I do it won't be intentional,' I reassure my voice quiet as she moves closer. Just a fraction. All this time I have been terrified of them. Never once did I consider they were equally terrified of me. This thought gives me hope. Yes, there are some who wish me nothing but harm. The realisation slams into me that they are the minority. Most of the population want nothing to do with all I represent.

'You are exquisite.' she cocks her head to study me. I pull out of my head and smile down at her.

'So are you,' I whisper. She isn't engineered but still beautiful. Perfect brows frame her green eyes. Porcelain skin stretched over delicate cheek bones. Her fuller bottom lip balances the cupid bow beneath a perfect straight nose. Her hair isn't limp like the other angry girl but tied back in an intricate braid.

'Thank you!' her voice soft, wistful. 'My mum, she worried about me. My sister she always tried to hide me. We are both clean though so she should have protected herself,'

'My Mother...' I hesitate, unsure how to phrase my thoughts. 'My Mother she thought I was too delicate for this.' My confession takes even me by surprise as I admit to my fragility.

'She will be looking for you,' Elle says her fingers brush my hair back from my face.

'No, she won't, I was being taken to Ireland,'

'Oh, you were with the United Human Federation then. They will want you back,' Her fingers release my hair and drift to my chest. My belly tightens with a feeling I haven't felt since being out here. I am attracted to her!

'They will?' My voice betrays my surprise as I clamp down on my body.

'Oh yes, my sister and I we were going to Ireland once we saved enough money.'

'You were? What's it like?' Any tiredness has gone away as I lean forward. It didn't occur to me that anyone would go there voluntarily.

'It is amazing. There isn't a breeding program, and they have men as well as Adams and I could meet one and fall in love. None of this matching business. You could be my husband if you wanted.' She looks at me all expectant and we giggle at that thought. She pulls a band from her wrist and runs her fingers through my hair tying it back from my face. She didn't ask and I don't mind.

'That is a lovely offer, but I have to do something before I can be anyone's husband,' I explain. I don't say anything more and I can see her expectant expression waiting for me to elaborate. Somehow, I don't want to share Aaron with them.

'Oh, an adventure. How exciting. You could be a noble and brave knight,' Her smile is a little forced once she knows I am not going to say anymore. She rummages in her pocket and pulls out a wrinkled sweet wrapper. 'A token my good knight,' she hands it to me with a giggle.

'Why thank you fair lady,' I reply and just for a moment we aren't sat on a cold concrete floor locked in a room. Only for a moment.

'Will you two go to sleep,' a grumpy voice complains. We look at each other and giggle again. Elle snuggles into me and dozes off as I sit holding her.

I startle awake as the door bangs open. My eyes wide as security flood inside.

'Wake up Elle,' pushing up I pull her sleepy form against

me. She stiffens against me as some of the girls scream as they are hauled to their feet.

'Where is the Adam?' One shouts as they push the girls toward the door.

'Here,' I step forward Elle pushed behind me.

'Move,' one shoves me hard making me stumble.

'Do not touch me,' I square up to the guard. She laughs as she grabs me and drags me out the room shoving me toward the others.

I am dragged through the building and outside. It's early and cold, the sun barely over the horizon. I shiver as I am pushed. Elle clings to my hand as the other girls silently follow. Her hand soft in mine as shivers make her body tremble as I pull her into me.

'It will be okay,' I reassure my arm around her.

'No, no it won't,' she sobs clinging to me.

I barely notice the girl sauntering toward us, swinging her hips seductively, my head still trying to deal with what happened in the street now I am outside again. How I am going to get out of this situation and save these girls.

'Hello, girls,' she drawls seductively, her chest only just held in by the dress she is wearing, which barely covers her bottom. To call it a dress is a massive exaggeration, in my opinion. The guards let go of me and smile at her, as she seems to purr around them, her perfume so strong I want to cough, as it cloys in my throat. Her hand brushes mine and she pushes something into my hand. I slip it into my pocket as she drapes her body around the guards.

'Get lost, slut,' one of the guard's growls, as the girl runs her hands over her.

'Oh, don't be like that, I might take offence,' she purrs again. They push her away and I glimpse red hair, Celina.

'Ooh, you have an Adam, let me touch him?' She pleads, trying to get near me.

'If you don't get lost, we will make you sorry,' the other guard growls, pointing her gun at the girl. I am dragged away to another building, trying to look back at the girl.

They walk us up some stone steps and in through some large doors. I get a brief look around as I am escorted up the stairs. I get the impression of neglect, much like the rest of the city. They pushed us into a room; They bang the door shut and I hear the clunk as it is locked. I lean against it and peer around the room; it is dark, just the glow of the street-lamp outside shedding light.

'Adam!' Elle's little voice has me pulling her close.

'It will be okay,' I reassure. Why I keep telling her this when there is nothing okay about this situation. As my eyes adjust to the gloom, I shuffle over to the bed and pull the paper from my pocket. It is crumpled, so I smooth it out. *Get to the art gallery. I will come for you, Celina*. I smile at this and then tare it into small pieces. I get to my feet and walk to the door I hope leads to the bathroom. I am relieved it does as I drop the pieces into the toilet, then flush it, watching as they swirl away. How the hell am I going to get to the art gallery? Did I want to get to the art gallery? This was my chance to strike out on my own again find Aaron.

The girls watch my every move huddled together. I amble around the room running my fingers against the wall as I think. Stopping at the window. Taking in my surroundings, this room is as neglected as the rest of the building, well the bits I have seen, anyway. Casting my gaze around the room, the carpet that was once a dark blue, faded, where the sun has bleached it through the window. There is no shade for the light fitting and the wallpaper is faded and peeling away from the wall. Apart from the bed, there is just a small table, scratched and ring marked where hot cups have been placed on it. The girls are huddled on the bed while they watch me.

The atmosphere is heavy with expectation and liberal amounts of fear.

Trying the door first. That is most definitely locked as I push my weight against it. Giving up on that, I move to the window and try it; it is a sash window. The paint is peeling and there is an orange mould kinda bubbling up from the wet wood; we had windows like this at the home, although they weren't rotten. Rotten my mind tumbles this word around as my eyes take in its every detail. Pulling my knife from my bag I dig it into the gap and run it around the window hopefully it will loosen. Dropping my knife back into my bag.

Reaching up, I undo the rusty catch, then give it an upward shove. I push up with all my strength, and to my utter amazement, it opens.

'What are you doing Boy,' Clara stalks over to me. She surveys the window and the small gap I have made. 'Well, I think I like your plan,' she smirks.

'You don't know my plan yet?' I raise a brow a cocky expression on my face. She gives a short chuckle.

'I can guess pretty boy. After all, neither of us fancy the alternative,'

'To damn right, no offence' I cross my arms over my chest.

'None taken,' she grunts, pushing me aside and shoving at the window.

'Gertie, give us a hand.' I glance over my shoulder as Gertie comes to my aid. She is considerably bigger than me in nearly every way.

Just a little at first, we give it another shove upwards. Looking out and down, I make the rash decision to climb out. Swinging my legs over the ledge, I sit for a minute.

'Adam, what are you doing?' Elle whisper shouts at me.

'Leaving,' I grin, cocking a brow at her. 'You coming,' I

wink. The other girls crowd around. Slowly, I turn and lower myself down, using the drainpipes clinging to the outside like strange metallic vines. Finally, letting go, I feel the relief as my feet touch the ground. Raising my arms, Beth lowers Elle. Catching her around the waist, I lower her down. The other girls followed her. Once down, they turn to me.

'Ladies, it was a pleasure,' I mock bow as Elle thumps me.

'Thanks Adam, you aren't as I expected,' Clara gives me a hug.

'Find happiness Clara,' I smirk as she glowers at me.

'You aren't coming with us?' Elle questions still holding my hand.

'No, you are safer without me,' my smile soft.

'Adam, thanks,' she reaches up and her lips press against mine. I respond my hands finding their way to her hair. Pulling away we catch our breath as we hold each other. Wow didn't expect that, my confused thought.

'Elle, we have to go,' Beth takes Elle and gently guides her away as I stand watching her disappear around the corner of the alleyway. Shouting breaks through the tumulus thoughts in my head. My feet start to jog as my survival instinct kicks in. Turning, they sprint along the alleyway.

I hear the door bang open and duck behind some dumpsters the smell of rotting food assaults my nostrils. I manage not to gag as I back into the shadow squatting down so as not to be seen. I watch as security rush out onto the street, stopping briefly, before splitting up to look for me, I assume.

I edge to the other side of the bins and then slip away along the now deserted street. I have been running for what seems like forever and I feel awful. Leaning over I throw up in the gutter. The adrenalin from the last few days wearing off. I stand up and wipe a shaking hand across my mouth and lean against the brickwork of the building. As I stand getting myself together, a shout starts directed at me, it seems.

'Oi, you, stay still,' one of the guard's shouts, and I hear pounding footfalls. Galvanising my legs into motion, I dart down an alleyway, ducking behind some large rubbish bins as the guards run past. I creep out and jog to the bottom of the alleyway. I stop for a fraction of a second, as indecision paralyses me and then I run again. I don't know where, I just must get away. I think I hear Celina's voice call my name. I am so scared, so keep running, the sound of gunfire in the distance. I see light coming from a doorway and duck inside, only to realise I am in a café. I shuffle to a table and sit down, picking up a menu, slowing my breathing.

'What do you want to order?' A sullen voice asks, startling me. Indecision swamps me. She will know I am a boy.

'Err, coffee… a mug of coffee, please and some toast,' I manage, not making eye contact with the girl. She slouches away and I breathe a sigh of relief. I pick up my bag and rummage in it for some money. The girl returns with my coffee and toast. I hand her my money. She stares. I know she knows. I try ignoring her and drink the coffee, scrunching up my face. It is disgusting. I reach for the sugar and tip loads into the mug, stirring it all the time, aware that she still stands watching me. Picking up a piece of toast, I take a bite, washing it down with coffee, my stomach settling.

'You… you are a boy, an Adam?'

'Sorry and your point is?' I answer, drinking my coffee, trying to sound nonchalant, as I try my level best to ignore her. A few drops of coffee spill onto the blue checked plastic cloth. In places it is white where it has been scrubbed.

'You shouldn't be here?' She answers unsure, she pulls out a chair and sits opposite me.

'Why not? This is a café, and I needed a coffee, so where else would I be?' I raise a brow at her and sip my coffee again. Taking in her appearance, she has red hair, but not like Celina's.

It doesn't look natural. To pink, I decide. My eyes travel down to the piercing in her nose, it makes her look scary, she is chewing gum and her apron doesn't look altogether clean, along with her hands with the chipped navy-blue varnish on her nails, all this filters through my brain in a matter of seconds.

'You aren't how I expected an Adam to be, I thought you are...' she gazes at me and bites her lip. I am intrigued now and put my mug down.

'How did you think I would be?'

'Dunno... different,' she shrugs again. 'You look awful. Where have you been? I mean, you are still amazing to look at, all perfect, an all,' she says quickly and blushes, as a quirky smile touches her lips, making her piercing glint in the light.

'Oh, um, the Madame had me, she wanted to, you know, with me,' I shrug, pushing my mug away and get ready to leave.

'Oh, that is nasty, she is well old, where are you going now you shouldn't be roaming the streets alone.'

'I am meeting someone at the art gallery, so I won't be on my own, but thanks for caring.' I smile at her as the lady on the table near the counter walks past me. She stops and glares at me, taking in every detail.

'Get out, you will get us killed,' she hisses, as I get to my feet.

'Mum, he is just a child,' the young girl behind her says, smiling at me. Her kind brown eyes survey me, and my face morphs into a smile, 'I have never seen a boy, you are lovely, not how I imagined,' she gazes at me and reaches up to touch my face, I flinch at her touch, 'Sorry,' she steps back, as her mother pulls her arm.

'We could hide him, keep him?' Someone speaks up. I look around to see who, but can't, as I am pulled back into my seat. The fact they didn't say safe hasn't escaped me. I am surrounded by people, and I can't see a way out. They debate what to do with me for a few more minutes.

'What, why?' The girl that served me frowns, not understanding, but I do perfectly, and this is an unwelcome development.

'He is very valuable. Why do you think he is hiding? He is being hunted.' an elderly well-dressed woman looks at me. 'Aren't you Adam, where is your Mother?' She waits for my answer, her watery blue eyes calculating. She doesn't know my name. She used the generic term for me, as I am not a person to her.

'I have been separated from her,' watching them all, I swallow down my fear calming my breathing. 'She will look for me.' I bluff, putting as much arrogance into my voice as the fear will allow. I glare at them all and reach for my coffee, taking a slurp, like I don't care, trying not to throw up as it is cold and disgusting.

'Who is hunting you?' The elderly woman asks gently, leaning forward slightly, to look at me. Someone else pulls the blinds down, so people outside can't look into the café, and I hear the clunk as the door is locked. Coffee slips down my throat and it is all I can do not to choke, as I am now trapped.

'Um, Gen-Corp, some security of the local Madame,' I shrug, cradling the mug in my hands, my posture casual, as if I am not intimidated by any of this. 'Um, pretty much everyone really.' I shrug again, pretending to drink some more of my coffee, feigning nonchalance, as I hear a collective hiss.

'That Adam will get us killed. Now let him leave please,' the mother says in a softer voice and a chorus of murmurs agrees with her.

'Sorry,' I mutter. The server unlocks the door and peers

out. Before opening it fully, she steps back, so I can step into the street. I stop when I feel her hand on my arm.

'Sorry,' she gazes at me; I smile like this is normal.

'Don't suppose you could point me in the right direction?' I smile again and she blushes.

'You really are beautiful! I never believed that you know.'

'Um, thanks… the art gallery?' I prompt.

'Oh, err, yeah, it's that way,' she points to my right, indicating which street I should head down. I nod my thanks and step through the door, onto the street. I look along the street and then walk for a bit, moving further into the town, walking as fast as I can. The shops are waking up as lights turn on and doors open. I don't want to be out here now as people appear.

CHAPTER 14

I stop to get my breath. I have no idea where I am, as I look around at all the elegant buildings. When I see the brass plaque that says the building is an art gallery, I feel relieved. I push the door open and walk in. No one stops me, or takes any notice of me, as I walk down the corridor. I shove my hands in my pockets and find myself in a large room; I stop in front of a Picasso and sit down on the bench, just to stare at it. With its bold colours and misplaced shapes, it is stunning.

I don't know how long I sit there before I realise no one is coming. Is that relief or regret? If she doesn't come, I can find Aaron as I planned. It disappointed the part of me that thought she cared. Of course, she didn't care I wasn't hers. I was just an inconvenience she had to sort out, the voice in my head, mocks. Pushing to my feet, I gather my things, pulling out my map so I can find the train station.

A voice over the tannoy announces they close in ten minutes. I amble through the various rooms and make my way outside. Someone brushes against me. I turn my head and glance at them, and then I look back at the exit sign, registering a dark face and chaotic frizzy hair, and loose baggy clothes.

'Adam,' my name, a whisper has my feet coming to a halt. Looking up, I immediately recognise the two girls now on either side of me.

'Clara, what are you doing here?'

'Collecting you,' she gives her signature smirk.

'Why?' I stumble forward as I squint in the cold gloom of twilight. This is the first sign they have herded me outside.

'Celina is otherwise detained, and we volunteered the other girl answers. Her piercing eyes bore into me. Her expression is a mixture of boredom and disdain.

'Where are we going?' I am not sure about this.

'A safe house until we can move you. Apparently, you are hot property,' she drawls, and I raise a brow.

'Who are We,' I air quote?

'The UHF, silly,' the girl rolls her eyes at me. 'Now hurry, it isn't safe out here for any of us,' We run down a couple of streets as the dark wraps around us. A hand on my chest stops my forward momentum.

'Shush,' Clara has I finger to her lips. My heart thumps. Now I am attuned to the sounds I can hear strange chattering mixed with manic laughter. I follow Clara's line of sight as they emerge from the gloom a group of ragged women. At first, I think their movements are random. The more I watch, I can see they are looking for something. They shuffle about the derelict buildings, touching, sniffing, and licking. It is quite disgusting in a fascinating way.

'What are they?' I whisper in Clara's ear.

'Mumbles, the infected. The original population well what's left.' I swallow down the fear she invokes. 'The vermin, if they find us, we are all dead,' she finishes. The sound of booted feet fills the night. Clara pulls me back.

'Damn, security doing a vermin sweep,' Clara swears in

annoyance. Turning, she grabs my hand and I notice the other girl has a gun in her hand. 'Let's go,' she pulls me back the way we came, turning down another street. I flinch as the sound of gunfire and screams rent the night apart. We stop against a building I say building loosely, as it has no roof and only three walls. Through the gaps in the brickwork, I can see bodies are in the street. A dark liquid runs in rivulets down the gutter. The rancid smell has my stomach heaving.

'Come on,' Clara pulls my hand, and we are running again. Turning down another street, I have a stitch in my side. We slow to a walk and the buildings here are intact. As I take in my surroundings, these buildings are elegant, cared for. A few have lights in the windows.

'Where are we going?'

'There is a safe house not far, we can sleep and get something to eat.'

'Will Celina be there?'

'No, but arrangements have been made to move you with us,' Clara pulls me up some steps and puts a code into a keypad. The door buzzes and she pushes it open, allowing the three of us to shuffle inside. Two uniformed guards greet us. They are not Gen-corp, so I relax a little.

'Miss Clara, you found him?' The guard's eyes slip over me, and I cast my eyes down my hands going behind my back. 'Oh, he is adorable,' the guard smiles.

'He is Madam Celina's. Just remember that' Clara snaps and takes my hand. Pulling me further into the house. 'You are just too damn pretty,' she mutters, and I want to laugh but I am afraid it will lead to breaking down as the adrenalin fades from my body.

'Where is Celina when will she get here?' I ask, my voice hopeful I don't feel altogether comfortable here.

'Sorry, she is in negotiations to get her boy. They want to trade you for him, and Celina is trying to prevent that,'

'Oh,' is all I manage. This place isn't safe either if that's the case.

'Adam,' turning to the voice as a small body wraps around me.

'Elle,' I gasp as I gather her up into my arms. Her lips are on mine in an instant. I moan and her tongue snakes into my mouth. I have never been kissed like this. My body comes to life, and I pull away before I embarrass myself. 'What are you doing here?' Wiggling to adjust myself.

'We got caught in vermin sweep but the UHF were there and took us under their care. Celina was distraught that you weren't with us when she realised, she couldn't get to the art gallery,'

'Are they really going to swap me for her match?'

'Not if she can help it, but it isn't just that,'

'Why what else is going on?'

'Well, Madame Trent is livid that we escaped with you and is combing the city for us. Madame Celina is trying to negotiate with her to get us out of the city,' Elle answered as she guided me further into the house. It wasn't like Madame Betties. This was more like the home they had kept me in. Wooden floor and cream walls, not homely. More functional. Ellie pushed a door open, and a cacophony of noise assaults me.

This room was obviously the kitchen. Steaming pans sat on the stove as people crowded around a table filling plates. Every available space was in use. All eyes turned to us and I duck my head.

'Are you hungry?' Elle grabs a plate and piles it with meat and potatoes and bread. Taking my hand, she drags me through the room and out another door. 'My room is this way,' she moves to the stairs, as I follow her, glad to be out the kitchen and away from all the people.

Elle's room was as functional as the rest of the house. It

has three beds in a row with cabinets between them. She plops down on the bed and indicates that I should follow.

'We will have to share,' she glances at me, and I shrug.

'Okay,' slipping my bag and coat off before undoing my laces and pushing my boots off, I curled my legs under me getting comfortable. Elle drew the curtain between us and the rest of the room. She then kicked off her shoes and snuggled into me. Placing the plate and two bottles of water between us.

'We should sleep,' Elle tidied our impromptu picnic away. She then strips down to her underwear before shuffling under the quilt. Hesitating, I do the same, letting her curl against me. Around us, I could hear the other occupants of the room moving around.

'Where is your sister?' Turning so I face her.

'In the kitchen with some other girls completing the plans for our move. She is part of the resistance. Has been all along never thought to mention that to me,' Elle's voice betrays her annoyance and anger. Pulling her close she doesn't resist I know what it is like to feel those you thought cared about you have in fact betrayed you. We snuggle together it is cold and the quilt is thin. In the silence, a bed creaks, followed by a sort of groan it seems so intimate.

'They are making love,' Elle whispers in the dark, her voice wistful. 'It is forbidden. Once we are taken to Ireland, they will be split up and found a male.' Elle's voice sounds sad.

'Do you have someone?' It occurs to me Elle may have lost more than her home.

'No, not anymore,'

'So, you have... made love.'

'Yes, but not with a male, obviously' she moves about so she is leaning up, looking at me. Her curtain of hair is a cocoon around our faces. Slowly, she leans down until our lips touch. She moves her leg over my thigh. My belly tightens and my body reacts to her touch. I break the kiss and try to move away.

'I ... I haven't been milked since being out here,' I can't stop the blush as embarrassment heats my skin.

'Hey,' her voice is gentle as her fingers run through my hair. 'I know how Adams work,' her smile is gentle as her eyes fix on mine.

'I know, I just,' my thoughts are a jumbled mess as this feeling of wanting to be close to her, touch her, is overwhelming every thought in my head. My chin wobbles, 'you don't want the mess,' my idiot brain blurts. Elle giggles and I manage a smile as she brushes my hair from my face.

'I know no one has touched you. Only used you. For that I am sorry,' her fingers brush through my hair. 'Let me give you this. Let me love you,' Her lips are on mine again, soft and demanding. I let out a groan, allowing her tongue to slip into my mouth. And it isn't an unpleasant sensation. She removes the last barrier between us, and I don't stop her. I don't want to stop her. I realise I want this.

'Relax,' she murmurs in my ear as she adjusts her position, and a gasp leaves my lips.

'You won't owe me anything. This is mutual,' her voice a whisper around us. Sucking in my bottom lip as I gaze up at her. Worry etched in my gaze.

'I can't protect you,'

'You don't have too. It won't be your responsibility I have my sister for that. I know you aren't for me, but...,' her fingers brush my lips releasing the lip I was worrying with my teeth. 'Let me love you just for tonight,'

'Yes,' I whisper giving her permission not that she needs it.

My hands are on her waist, my eyes are wide as I swallow. Elle lets out a whimper and bites her lip. She takes my hands from where they are squeezing her hips. Positioning them on either side of my head, our fingers entwine. Her gaze holds mine. Then she slowly moves. She shows me where to touch her. Bringing us to a peak of pleasure. She swallows my groan as she pants my name.

I lay languid limbs entwined. Wiping my sweat-soaked hair from my eyes. Elle is breathing hard as she lays her head on my chest. Her eyes are closed, but her lips are smiling. I drift to sleep only to be woken by her hands and mouth.

'Elle,' her name is forced through my lips on a moan as her hands reach up and pull my head down so her mouth can plunder mine. My body buried in hers. Light filters through the curtain as the other occupants of the room stir. Her body drags the last pleasurable shudders from mine as we slump in a sweaty heap. I have lost count of the times she woke me, or I woke her. When I next wake, she is gone.

I amble downstairs. Having showered and dressed, the house is silent. The girls have gone, including Elle. Somehow, I know I won't see her again. Pushing the kitchen door open, I hesitate as I take in the scene before me. A group of soldiers stand around holding steaming mugs. One detaches from a group and smiles at me.

'Adam, you are up good,' she passes me a steaming mug and I am grateful to find tea. Sinking onto a chair, I try my best to ignore the curious glances directed at me.

'Did you sleep well?'

'Yes, thank you.' a plate with a bacon sandwich is pushed toward me as a large fluffy ginger cat rubs around my legs before hopping onto my lap. I run my fingers through its soft fur. A rumbling purr emits from it. I have never seen a real cat before and he is everything I hoped it would be. Pleasure lights up my features a few of the soldiers smile while watching our interaction.

'Adorable,' someone murmurs.

'Marge, get down you monster,' hands take hold of the cat and remove it from my lap.

'She only wants your bacon,' the soldier holding the cat chuckles as she pushes the cat out a window. The cat meows mournfully from the windowsill before flicking its ginger tail and saunters off.

'Right when you have finished that they instructed us to deliver you to Madame Celina,'

'Oh, I thought I was going with the girls?'

'No to dangerous I am afraid,' I am disappointed in a relieved sort of way.

CHAPTER 15

*T*rudie, that's the name of the soldier who is escorting me. Her friendly smile and dark frizzy hair all combine to relax me. She chatters away next to me quite unsoldierly. I don't mind. It gives me time to sort through last night in my head. I know I will not see Elle again. Somehow, I don't mind that. Yes, I am sad but like she said I am not for her, and she isn't for me. Trudie was at the art gallery. I remember her chaotic hair. Trudie inspects me as I do my coat up. 'Got everything?' She enquires.

'Yes, thank you,' shouldering my bag as nerves twitch my stomach.

'You are so cute and polite.'

'Thanks, I think,'

'Just love your non name,' she quips.

'Non-Name,' I frown, and she laughs.

'Yeah, its genius,' she pulls the door open as I chuckle. If that was her way of relaxing me, it worked.

Trudie turns and locks the door. She takes my hand in her firm grasp as we descend the steps to the street. Stopping on the pavement, she turns to me. Adjusting my clothing, her fingertips brush my cheek.

'You will be okay, Adam,' she whispers. 'Just trust Celina, she will take care of you,'

'Thank you.' I take a deep breath as Trudie turns and we saunter along the street. A few people pass us, but none pay us any attention hurrying about their business. They on the other hand fascinate me. There nondescript clothing an obvious camouflage. I want to know where they go. What they do?

Taking in the rows of houses set back from the street that is lined with trees. The occasional horse and cart trundles by piled with stuff covered by tarpaulin. My eyes wide as I take it all in. I turn trying to see everything.

'Adam, concentrate you will attract unwanted attention,' her hand on my arm propelling me forward again.

'Sorry,' I apologise. Trudie is on alert to danger her pistol in her hand concealed. I notice the lack of voices.

I didn't hear the shot, I just felt the jerk of Trudy's hand, as she crumples to the ground. The once drab, grey pavement, now splattered with the bright crimson of her blood. I feel the heat of my silent tears running down my cheeks. Trudie lies motionless, her now glassy lifeless eyes staring unseeing at the beautiful clear blue sky as her blood pools on the pavement, purple, grey chunks of brain and flecks of bone floating in it. I feel vomit welling up in my throat at the sight of it and must turn away from the grizzly sight. I turn my head to one side and vomit, wiping my mouth with the back of my hand.

I sit for a bit, too scared to move, unsure where the shot came from. Only knowing there are booted feet approaching me, I still cannot move. I hear shouting and more gunfire; I shiver, but still, I can't move.

'Adam, get up, now,' Celina shouts at me.

'Ce... Celina, she is dead,' I stutter, as shock sets in.

'Yes Adam, and if you don't get up now, we will be as well,' Celina grabs my arm, forcing me to my feet, she pulls me away from Trudie's body and drags me along the street, pulling me into a doorway as security runs pass, followed by more gunfire. I can hear sirens blaring now.

'Who will feed her cat?' Is the only thing I can mumble. Celina frowns at me in confusion.

'It's routine vermin sweep. Trudie was bringing you to me. You annoyed the Madame by escaping and taking her girls with you.' She peers around the edge of the doorway. 'I annoyed the madame by not dying,' Celina shrugs while checking out the street. I just stand there trying to comprehend that statement while keeping it together.

'Come on, I have Bob hidden close.' I nod in a daze and meekly follow her, my brain in freefall. I can't cope anymore. We arrive at the stable, and I sink onto a bale of straw.

'I can't do this,' the sob that escapes. I can't stop or the tears that follow as I just sort of break. Embarrassingly, I can't stop the deluge of tears. I mean I have cried before, I do it a lot but usually I don't have an audience and certainly not in front of Celina.

'No, Adam, that is not an option, do you understand?' She states, wrapping her arms around me, as sobs rack my whole body.

'Why?' I glare at her, clenching my fists, my feet apart as my entire posture goes ridged.

'Why, what?'

'Why is that not an option? I am so tired Celina. I couldn't bear it if they hurt you or killed you. Maybe you should exchange me for your Adam,' I state firmly, holding eye contact with her. I can see colour staining her cheeks as my words sink in.

'No...no that isn't happening. I made my position quite

clear your freedom isn't up for negotiation do you understand?' She steps back. Her arms dropping from where they were wrapped around me, her stance menacing.

'But it is all my fault he isn't here now,' I wipe my face on my sleeve before crossing my arms over my chest.

'No, it isn't. They should have been paying attention to you. That's their job to take care of you,' she answers vehemently. 'Your Mother should have been honest with you. Damn it, the mistakes made regarding you are ridiculous,'

'But you nearly died. We both almost did. You should give me back,' I say my voice sombre.

'Oh, so you want to die at twenty do you,' she snaps back. Confrontation really isn't my thing, but I feel I should make an exception.

'Better than dying at seventeen,' I bark.

'Whatever, idiot, hand yourself in,' she snorts in disgust. Great, she isn't intimidated by me at all, well that's typical. I huff as my fists shake and I clench my teeth.

'I am not a child,' I shout back.

Well, stop behaving like one then,' she shouts, her hands on her hips as she glares at me. Well, that stung, and I am at a bit of a loss now. I am taken by surprise when she laughs; I glare at her and then my lips twitch up and I laugh.

'You are such an idiot,' she is still laughing.

'You bloody lost me.' I say through the sobs and giggles.

'Yeah, sorry about that.' She pulls me to her and wraps around me hugging me hard. 'I won't again promise,' her lopsided smile reassures me as I wipe the tears and snot from my face onto my sleeve.

'Good,' is all I can say.

It is late evening, the gathering dusk shrouding everything in shadows. We turn off the road and make our way down a long, tree-lined farm road. I can just see the chimney stacks of the house we are heading for. Bob trots down the drive, and I perk up at the thought of not sleeping in the tent.

The house comes into view surrounded by trees. It is large, built of grey stone with ivy growing over it. I can imagine it bustling with people and activity, but now it appears deserted and silent. I had assumed someone would wait anxiously for us to arrive; I voice my fear.

'Celina, it's silent, shouldn't there be people?' I feel Celina tense as she scans the outhouses and barns.

'Well, let's go to the stables first, sort out Bob and then investigate the house.' Celina tightens her arm around me. 'It will be alright, Adam.'

'You think,' I mutter. Something is wrong. My stomach twists as the nerves take hold. No offence to Celina, but I doubt she could protect me if people from Gen-Corp and the Adam program are here to collect me, if they have somehow found me.

Celina unloads Bob and removes his saddle and tack. Picking up the brush, I brush Bob; I find it calms me. I like Bob and I think he likes me; he nudges me with his nose, as I finish brushing him. Celina passes me Bob's food and I feed him, patting him. Celina watches me, she has that indulgent look on her face, my Mother sometimes had when she watched me doing something clever.

The look from Celina feels slightly patronising and it annoys me. I am in a bad mood today and I'm not sure why. Well, apart from seeing someone shot dead in front of me. Celina is just annoying me.

'It too quiet can't you go and check the house or something,' I'm being horrid, I know that, so I attempt to smile at her.

'Yeah, it is, but I am not leaving you here so I will wait,' she snaps back.

'Yeah whatever,' I put away Bobs things.

'Adam, it's alright we can sneak in and see what's going on. If there's a problem we leave, okay.' I watch as Celina walks over to me, she pulls me into a hug. I awkwardly put my arms around her, congratulating myself for not flinching. Stepping back slightly, her arms still around me, she gazes at me intently. My arms drop to my sides, biting my lip. I don't like this uncertainty. What does she want? Am I meant to say or do something? Why is she just looking at me? I am not very good at reading people. Mathew always used to say that was why I was so socially inept. Her soft lips touch mine. Whoa, not what I was expecting. It is kinda nice though. What do I do? This is Celina. She moves closer, nibbling my lip and my damn body reacts. I pull back, engulfed by embarrassment? I don't want this with Celina I thought we had established that.

'What did you do that for?' I ask, a bit abruptly turning away so I can adjust myself, not wanting her to know I am no better than an animal.

'I thought... well, never mind, I can see you are in a mood this afternoon.' She shrugs.

'I am not in a mood, well yeah, I am, and wouldn't you be if you were in my position?' I add, running my hands through my hair, a nervous action. I look at her. Celina's eyes cast down and there is a slight tinge of pink on her cheeks. I can see I have upset her by the downturn of her mouth. Oh damn, I am going to have to apologise. Wait, I don't want to apologise. She's the one who kissed me.

'Sorry,' Celina mumbles, and moves slightly away from me, putting fresh hay in the rack for Bob.

'Celina, sorry, it's just....' I hang my head as I try to assemble an explanation. 'The last few days have been traumatic,' I try to apologise, but where we seemed quite close. Celina now appears distant as she stands, saying nothing and avoiding my gaze. In silence, I leave the stables.

I walk up to the house. Although it is getting dark, the lights are off, and the curtains are open. There doesn't seem to be any movement within. I get to the front door and reach for the handle. In the time I take to hesitate to turn the handle, Celina has caught up with me, her shiny silver pistol drawn.

'Stay behind me,' she orders, and any meekness she had from before has gone. We step into the house, and I cringe as my boots clack on the stone tiles. The surrounding air feels damp and cold, no welcoming warmth; The hairs on the back of my neck and arms rise as the cold air brushes my skin.

Tentatively, I walk forward, clenching my teeth as I shiver. From the cold or nerves, it's hard to tell as goose bumps rise on my skin. I glance up the long sweeping staircase and advance toward another door in front of me. I push it open and find myself in a large kitchen. My shoulders relax, easing the built-up tension within me. It's obvious that someone has been here recently. The surfaces are free of dust and the room looks clean.

I place my knife and bag on the table. I can hear Celina opening and shutting doors as she investigates the other rooms on the ground floor. Opening the fridge, I peer inside. It's well stocked and fresh.

'At least the fridge isn't empty,' I call out.

'Which means someone was here!' Celina comments as she enters the kitchen. I open a door I assume will lead outside or to a little closet. It is a closet and is more spacious than it appears from the outside, with more than enough space to store the four bodies carelessly dumped on the floor.

'Oh, my God! This cupboard's full of dead people!' Recoiling, I take a minute to calm my heart rate.

'Step back, let me see,' she orders as she pushes pass me to peer into the cupboard. 'They're from the United Human

Federation, I sent them here to wait for us. We shouldn't stay here long, and we really shouldn't look in that cupboard again.' She smirks as she closes the door.

'Considering it's a cupboard full of corpses, you're taking it very well.' I respond, slightly disgusted at Celina's casual acceptance of such a macabre sight.

'Meh, you're in the real-world honey, folk die all the time out here. Look on the bright side, at least we know where everyone went,' Celina replies, her arm going around my waist as she steers me away.

'Well, what about the person who murdered them? They might still be around,' I sort of know her reaction was to reassure me, but it didn't work, and I am far from reassured.

'If it was Gen-Corp, they would still be here. It was probably travellers or raiders looking for food or anything of value. Probably just passing through. I doubt they'll be back,' she responds casually.

'If they didn't plan on hanging around, why move the bodies? I somehow doubt they killed all the occupants while they were collectively in this cupboard. Did they?' I ask, pushing my hands in my pockets, feeling them shake. I keep staring at the door, imagining the corpse's lifeless eyes staring back at me.

'Come on, Celina, let's just go,' I whine, picking up my things from the table and walking over to Celina to take her hand.

'No, Adam, it's late and dark. We will have to stay here. Besides, Bob needs a proper night in a stable, with fresh hay and water.'

'But what about the dead people? What if whoever killed them comes back and gets us too?' I ask, pulling down the blind on the window so I can't see outside. My whole body is stiff, and I feel a little sick just thinking about the sort of people that did this.

'The food is still fresh, not to mention the bodies. Whoever killed them might still be around, in which case we will be far safer in a nice sturdy house than out there in a tent,' she reasons calmly.

'Alright fine, but can we search the house some more first, please?'

I gingerly climb the stairs with Celina following. We search the upstairs, but that is deserted as well. Why kill those people and just leave? It makes little sense. As far as I can see, nothing has been stolen. I have a bad feeling about this, but Celina is right. I'd rather fight off a murdering psycho in here than out in that dingy tent.

'Celina, where are the rest of your people? I thought that there would be more than four?' I watch her as she surveys the room, opening the wardrobe, and the door leading to the adjoining bathroom.

'No, this was just a safe house, a staging place to build you up for the rest of the journey. I know how hard this is for you to adjust to being free.' She shuts the doors and looks at me.

'Oh,' is all I can think of as a response. The room we have settled in has a fireplace and bathroom. I really don't want to be wandering around at night. I get the fire going to warm up the room and it helps to distract me from the uneasy feeling still festering at the back of my mind. Celina has drawn the curtains. Which helps to keep the room warm.

'Come on, you will feel better when you have eaten,' Celina guides me to the stairs.

'Are you cooking then because I have no experience with cooking?' I peer at her as we descend the stairs.

'Well yeah, you have no experience period,' her face crumples into a smile and she lets out a chuckle.

'How rude,' Celina playfully punches my arm, lifting the mood.

We relocate to the kitchen, where Celina cooks some of the food from the fridge. I sit at the table and try not to think about the bodies. 'Did you know them?' I ask after a moment of silence.

'Not personally, no, they probably just lived here,' she replies as she cuts some chicken breasts from the fridge.

'Who do you reckon killed them?'

'Dunno, but whoever it was ain't here now, so quit worrying.' She puts her casserole dish in the oven.

'Well, what if they come back?'

'So, what if they do? I've got all the welcome they'll ever need right here.' Celina fingers her holstered pistol with a grin.

'I know, I wouldn't want to tangle with you,' I reply, as Celina bustles around the kitchen tidying and washing her utensils. This amuses me, and I can't help but chuckle.

'What's so funny?' She raises an eyebrow at me.

'Nothing, well you I guess,' I smile again.

'We should make use of everything while we're here,' she mumbles and goes back to her cooking, peeling vegetables.

It smells delicious, some sort of chicken in a tomato sauce. I watch as she mashes the potatoes and then dishes up.

'What happened you know, when I lost you?' She doesn't look at me, just casually eats her dinner but that question wasn't casual, no it was far from casual.

'She– she killed them all, Celina,' devastation swamps me again.

'I know and I am sorry you had to see that,' Celina reaches for my hand and gives it a squeeze as I manage a wobbly smile.

'She held us in this run-down house. Me and those girls. I climbed out a window and helped them escape. Didn't know which way to go and sort of ended up in this café with all these people. Do you know they discussed selling me? While

I was there, can you believe that, like that was all I was, just a commodity,' I say with indignation, and eat some of my chicken.

'My god Adam, what were you thinking, that was very dangerous,' Celina looks at me.

'Well, yeah, they wanted to sell me. I was being chased at the time by security, I didn't do it out of choice.' I reply, feeling hurt. She seems to have missed the point. I huff and eat the rest of my dinner. We eat in silence, and I try to help Celina tidy up, but I seem to hinder her more than help. I feel exhausted now I have eaten and make my excuses to go to bed. Celina smiles at me and gets up to follow me. She obviously doesn't want to stay downstairs with the dead bodies. I don't blame her. I wouldn't want too either.

'I'm going to have a bath, don't know when I will get the chance again,' she disappears into the adjoining bathroom as I get undressed and curl up in the enormous bed. I listen to the water running and a sweet flowery smell drifts into the bedroom. Celina must have found some bath oil. I hear the splosh as she gets in and her sigh of contentment. Yawning deeply, I roll over and close my eyes. Thinking about Ellie and where she is. If she is safe. I think about the kiss Celina gave me and if she wants to do with me the thing I did with Ellie. I hope not I am not attracted to Celina like I was to Ellie.

I am awake to Celina on her phone again talking. 'Thom... Yeah... No, they are all dead. What the hell is going on? It freaked him right out... Okay... But this is getting difficult, and I will need an extraction team... Yeah... Well, he isn't your average robust Adam.... I don't know he's different... he's delicate feminine even... No not likely, I like him, must have something about him to escape few do that, he knows about his fate... yeah he isn't like other Adams I have met... he says he is looking for someone... another Adam from what I could get out of him... that in its self is unusual they don't normally form bonds like that,... he is bright, not dumbed down like other Adams, doesn't need to please either, yeah we can stay here one more day, Yeah pull his file, number 689302, I have a feeling about this, Thanks, Thom and Thom sorry about your soldiers.'

I hear her drop the phone and I wonder who Thom is or even who she is. Delicate? Feminine? The cheek of it! I huff again and turn over, my bad mood returning. When did she take my number? Turning my wrist, I gaze at it for a moment before pulling the sheet to cover it. I wish Ellie were here she would get me out of my bad mood. I realise I miss her.

Celina slips back into the room 'I know you're awake,' she jabs me as she climbs into bed.

'I am now,' I complain, rolling over to look at her. 'Who were you talking to?'

'A colleague of mine from the UHF' she replies.

'What's their name?'

'His name is Thom, not that it is much of your business,' she replies cagily.

'It is if you are planning on handing me over to him.'

'What if I am? What's saying that is a bad thing?' The irritation in her voice growing.

'I'm not saying that it is necessarily a bad thing, but if I am going to have no say over my future, I would at least like to know what it is likely to be.' I am annoyed at her obtuse behaviour.

'Look, Adam, you're right. You don't really get a say over what your future will be. It sucks for you, but that is just the way it is. Luck of the draw, I'm afraid and I certainly didn't make it that way. It has been that way since the moment you were born into the Adam program. It's sad and inhumane that you have no control over your own destiny, but that is the way it is under Gen-corp. Don't you get that?' She says, staring me hard in the eyes.

'Of course, I get that. Why do you think I escaped?' I snap back angrily, 'But what was the point of escaping if I am trading imprisonment with them for imprisonment with you?'

'Ugh, Adam, learn to trust me! The UHF doesn't want to imprison you! We fight against Gen- Corp, we want to free the Adams and overthrow them. But until that happens, there are certain harsh realities you will have to face and learn to live with, one of them being the fact that from now on you will have to stay with the UHF if you want to survive.'

I sigh, momentarily defeated. 'Fine, but you know that this arrangement is not permanent.'

'Fine whatever, once we link up with the rest of the UHF and sort everything out you will be free to do what you want.' Celina replies before turning away from me and reaching into her bag sat on the floor beside the bed. She pulls an old hardcover book out and starts reading, her face set in a scowl.

After a while, my curiosity gets the better of me, and I must ask. 'What you reading?'

'My book.'

'Well, yeah, I can see that. What is it about?'

'It's about this girl who falls in love with this boy, but she has to prove to him she is his equal.' Frowning, I gaze at Celina. I didn't understand any of that.

'Why? He should prove himself to her.'

'No, this is an old book about how relations between the sexes used to be.'

'Oh.'

'Read this, it might help?' She passes me the book open at the relevant page, a huge grin on her face.

My eyes scan the page, raising an eyebrow at what it is suggesting. I have read nothing like this, 'Celina?'

'Hmm,'

'This is an illegal text, isn't it?' I glance at her.

'Yeah,' biting her lip, her eyes trained on my face.

'You know what it is suggesting is illegal?' I put the book down and focus on her.

'I know but it is so romantic, all proper love, not like now.' her voice is wistful as her features soften. 'Don't know why I am discussing this with you anyway,'

'Elle was all romantic and stuff,' I say handing back her book. Trying not to be hurt by her words.

'Elle? Was she one of the girls you escaped with?'

'Yeah, she wanted to get to Ireland to fall in love,' Would she have loved me if I had gone with her? Did I want that? Celina snaps her fingers in front of my face. 'What,' I grumble.

'You checked out then,' Celina raises a brow before she goes back to her book. 'Did you like this, Elle?'

'Yeah, I did,' I confess. 'Well, according to your book, I should be in charge of telling you what to do,' I finally answer, putting her book down, trying my best not to laugh.

'Oh, yeah, like that is going to happen.'

'Just saying if you want me to love you,' I deadpan, trying not to laugh. She leans over and snatches up her book and picking up a pillow. She hits me with it while I laugh.

'Oh, go to sleep! As if I want your love.'

***

I WANDER DOWNSTAIRS to find Celina making porridge; she divides it between two bowls and passes one to me along with a cup of tea.

'Thanks, so what's the plan?' I ask, tucking into the porridge. It is thick and tasteless, but I don't complain.

'We move to the next location and hope they are alive,' she sits opposite me, eating her porridge.

'Is it far?'

'No, but the thing is, it won't be like the town, it will be…' she pauses and looks me over.

'It will be what?' I demand, feeling nervous.

'Well, it won't be controlled. It will be wilder, although it is policed but not in a good way,' she finishes.

'The puppies,' I mumble, pushing away my bowl and sipping my tea.

'Yeah, the puppies, but it isn't just them you are so valuable and people well they aren't just scared they are desperate, you, well you represent the control Gen-Corp has over their lives,' she shrugs as she gazes at me biting her bottom lip again.

'Yeah, I got that in the café,' is all I can manage. 'They weren't common, the people in the café, they were ordinary,' I muse out loud.

'They still wanted you though.'

'Yep, when they realised what I was, they discussed keeping me, selling me, you know, that sort of thing.' I shrug at her incredulous look.

'Jeez, Adam.'

'I think they were curious more than anything, the girl serving. I talked to her a lot; she was nice. They had never seen an Adam. I was scared, but I am not sure they would really hurt me.' I shrug.

'Are you mental, of course they would?'

'You think. That wasn't the impression I got.'

'Trust me, Adam, finding you would be like all their dreams coming true,' Celina crosses her arms over her chest and glares at me.

'Yeah, so you say,' I mumble back. I hate the way she is so superior sometimes.

'Oh, if you are going to sulk, I am going to see to Bob,' she gets up, scrapping her chair on the floor. I am not sulking.

'Celina, I um have to find my brother,' I look at her, trying to read her expression. It is neutral, which I find odd. I had expected some sort of reaction. Most people laugh and then call me stupid.

'I know you do,' she finally says, gazing at me.

'You do,' I hold her gaze, waiting for her to say something; I can clearly see she is thinking over what I have said as she is chewing her bottom lip.

'It is very unusual for an Adam to have a sibling,'

'Yeah, I know. I think that is why they split us up and then lied to me, I suspect they told him the same lie,' I shrug and pull my gaze from hers as I can feel the sting of tears and I don't want to cry. 'I need to see him, if only to say goodbye. We didn't... I woke up, and he was gone.' I sniff and dash at my eyes with the heel of my hands.

'Oh, Adam,' she moves round to where I am sitting. She gazes at me, and I nod. She wraps her arms around me in a hug and kisses my cheek. I feel all warm inside and it isn't from that porridge. I smile and tentatively kiss her cheek back.

'Right, you stay here, make the tea, while I feed Bob, okay?' She stands up and looks at me, grinning. 'When I come back, we can plan our next move and decide what to do.'

'Okay,' I grumble. I don't like her leaving me. It makes me feel vulnerable.

'I won't be long,' she gives me a smile before she leaves the room. I hear her clatter through the house and the door bang. I do as she says and wash up the breakfast things. Then go about making the tea. I like this, doing stuff. We weren't allowed to do anything domestic in the home. I am so engrossed; I don't notice the sound of the front door opening.

Suddenly, the door bursts open, and three dirty women barge in. I grab my knife turning to face them. The women give a collective laugh and advance closer. The knife in my hand didn't seem to deter them.

'Well, well, what do we have here?' The biggest one advances toward me; her lips peel back in a smile, revealing several teeth missing; I gag on the smell. 'A missing Adam,' she reaches out her hand to take the knife from me. I swing it defensively, cutting her hand and causing her to recoil. She smiles and licks the blood from her wound. 'My, my, he's a feisty one, isn't he?' She smirks as the other two and approach me. With my attention focused on her, I don't notice one of the other two, the scrawny one, sneak around behind me. She grabs me from behind. The fat one moves with athletic grace, snatching the knife from my hand.

'Get off me!' I yell as her other hand grabs my jumper and pulls me close to her, forcing the scrawny one to release me. I gag as her fetid breath wafts up my nose and fills my mouth; she smiles a repulsive toothless grin as she drops the knife.

'Let me touch him, Gina, I ain't never seen an Adam,' the scrawny, equally dirty woman moves to my side. She reaches out her hand and strokes my face. 'Isn't he pretty?'

'Get off, I found him first,' the one called Gina bats the other woman away, sending her sprawling. The third woman is cleaner than the first two and she just stands against the wall watching me with her small bird-like eyes, making me realise she is the dangerous one. I pray Celina would come back, but wasn't sure what she would do against these three.

'That's enough,' she pushes away from the wall and walks toward me. She barges the other two out of the way and stands in front of me. 'Madame Trent, will pay well for you, we were right to come back here!' she takes my face in her hand and turns my head inspecting me, with my hands free I punch her as hard as I can in the stomach, she grunts and lets go of me, I lurched for the knife and sweep it off the floor into my hand waving it in front of me again as I back to the door.

'Stop him, you idiots,' the one I had just punched growls as I duck. A fist swings toward my head, narrowly missing me. I am nearly at the door as the one called Gina moves with agile speed, for someone so clumsy looking. Rushing at me, shoving me hard into the wall, my head connecting with the door frame, stars exploded before my eyes, as my legs crumple followed by darkness.

CHAPTER 16

'Boy, wake up,' someone lightly slaps my face.

'Don't... feel good.' my arms are forced into my coat and my bag pushed over my head. I can hear shouting and gunfire; it all seems so far away. I just can't focus. My shoulders protest as my arms are pulled back and bound. I still can't get my brain to function. I need to run away, escape.

'Need to leave now, boy,' her voice urgent as my legs sag and darkness invades my vision.

'Celina, I... I need to find her,' my voice slurs as I try to remain conscious.

The urge to throw up wakes me, as something cold is pressed to my head. It feels nice as I slip back into unconsciousness. Voices wake me, along with the pain in my head, which I must admit is extraordinary. Can't say if I have ever felt this much pain before. If I have, the only assumption I can come up with is my mind blocked it out. Someone lifts my shoulders and places a cup to my lips as water trickles down my throat, some dribbles down my chin onto my shirt. My brain registers that my wrists are still bound.

'Celina?' I mumble, as pain crashes through my head.

'Shush, boy, go to sleep.'

'Who are you?

'Sophie, you sleep, I get dinner, you are safe now, boy.'

Turning, my arm is numb where I am laid on it. The slight movement makes me want to throw up as my head pounds. No idea where I am and frankly don't care. If I died now, it would be alright, is my last coherent thought.

Pain wakes me; lying still so I can concentrate on my body. Apart from my head, nothing else hurts, so that must be good. A damp musty air surrounds me along with the smell of a fire which I assume is the source of the warmth. I wonder where I am. It occurs to me I could open my eyes, wasn't there someone here earlier talking to me.

Slowly, I pry my eyes open. I am alone and not outside, but not in the house, either. I appear to be in a cave. How the hell did I get here? Moving my legs to get up proves to be a bad idea as my head swims with pain and the urge to be sick overwhelms me. Lying down again, squeezing my eyes shut, I try to control the pulsating headache. I give my wrists a wriggle to see if I can get loose. Not a chance damn it.

I hear footsteps, pretending to be asleep. What do I do if it's those women? I swallow, squeezing my eyes tight. Opening one eye, I watch as a small, pale girl enters the cave. She has two birds in her hand hanging lifeless, upside down, their feet between her fingers.

'You awake, boy,' she says as she sits by the fire and goes about removing the feathers from the birds. I open both eyes and can now see the birds are pheasants.

'Yeah,' I manage, 'Where are the other women?' I ask.

'They went, I scare them away cos they stupid,' she goes back to her task, laughing to herself. Oh great, a crazy person has captured me, Celina, where are you!

'I am with someone. She will look for me,' I say after a while and open my eyes. I instantly regret opening them as she takes a knife and chops up the two birds in front of me. The blood and the stench are revolting. I look away to keep from retching.

'You mean the girl with red hair? She was stupid as well.' She puts the pheasant meat in a pot hanging over the fire and stirs its contents. All the while chuckling to herself. She stands up and walks over to me and squats down in front of me. 'You are mine now and we have babies.' she reaches out her filthy blood smeared hand and runs her fingers down my face.

'Please don't touch me!' Tears spring to my eyes from the pain.

'You hurt.'

'Yes.'

'I help you; you sit up and drink this,' she takes hold of me and pulls me up none too gently, Florence Nightingale she ain't. She passes me a chipped mug with some brown liquid in it. 'Drink!', She stares at me, as she lifts it to my lips. It is horrible and very bitter. I screw my face up and swallow it down.

'Oh, yuk,' I see her grin at my reaction.

'Willow bark, make you better,' she gets up and goes back to her cooking. 'Need you better if I want you to give me a baby,' she nods at me before moving away. I do not want to give her a baby. That I am sure of.

'Where is this place?' The smell of her stew permeates the air.

'Place to hide, won't find us here,' her voice sounds sad as she collects two bowls from a shelf. She is very poised and athletic.

Her clothes all seem too big on her. From the brown baggy trousers, held up by a string belt, to the shirt tied at her waist, the sleeves rolled up. Her discarded boots and coat by the door.

'Do you hide often?' She fascinates me, she is nothing like Celina. Sophie is small and delicate, almost birdlike in her fragility. Her pale-yellow hair is tied back, and her blue eyes are almost too large for her face. Giving her a vulnerable, innocent look.

'Sometimes,' she stalks over to me. In her hand a large knife. I shrink back.

'Running would be stupid,' she says cutting the cable tie around my wrist. I rub them as she steps away. Am I her prisoner?

This makes me want to know who she hides from! Who could threaten her, the United Human Federation, maybe, because she wants to steal one of their Adams, or Gen-Corp, for the same reason! She dishes the stew up into the bowls and moves over to sit next to me, passing me one.

'You talk too much. You need to learn to be quiet.' Eating the stew, I mull over her words. Never thought I talked too much! The other boys used to complain I was too quiet.

'Why did you capture me?'

'I want a boy. I saw you in the snow, running.'

'How, why?'

'They were moving out retired Adams. I was going to take one. They careless and stupid.'

'I am not retired.'

'I know I saw you run. You different, I like that. Lost you in the town had to wait for federation girl to move you again knew she would, knew where as well.' her smile is triumphant.

'Oh, Sophie, if they catch us, they will kill you.'

'Maybe, have to catch me first,' the smirk on her face gives her a cheeky look, and it is all I can do not to smile back.

'What if I don't want to go with you?' She gives me a look. Sort of puzzled and menacing at the same time. I realise I am far from safe with this odd little girl.

'You sleep, we move tomorrow,' She squats behind me pulling my arms behind my back. The bite of a cable tie irritates my already chaffed skin. Well that answered my question.

'You don't have to tie me up,' I gaze into her eyes. She bites her lip, and it is the first bit of indecision I have seen from her.

'Yes, don't trust boy,' She moves away from me with one last glance.

Shuffling down, I shut my eyes, finding sleep easily. In the night, I am aware of her wrapped around me. I don't object, even though that is probably stupid as I don't know her, but something about her appeals to me. She has a vulnerability that resonates within me and reminds me of Ellie.

I wake to the smell of stew; I push myself up with only a dull pain in my head.

'Sophie please can you untie me I won't run,' she turns to me her eyes appraise me before stalking over. 'Thank you,' our eyes lock. She cuts the ties and shoves them in her pocket.

'Don't run,' she mutters as she stalks away.

I find my boots and pull them on and do them up. I see my bag near to me and I pull it over, rummaging inside until I locate my toothbrush and paste. I retrieve the bottle of water from my bag, heading outside shivering as the wintry morning air wraps around me and I regret not putting my coat on.

Glancing around, I see the faint path through the wood and scrub behind a sheer cliff. The valley carved by the snaking river, mist drifting like steam, reminding me of another river, another time. When Aaron was still with me, and the milking hadn't started. Pushing that memory away and quickly cleaning my teeth, it immediately makes me feel better, the horrible taste gone from my mouth. The knife at my throat and her body pressed to mine has me freezing.

'I said don't run,' her warm breath fans my ear.

'I...I haven't,' I stutter out.

'What you doing?' She lowers the knife and steps back. A breath I was holding mists in the frigid air.

'Cleaning my teeth,' holding up my toothbrush I notice the tremor to my hand.

'Hmph,' She stalks away. I gather my things once she has gone. I try to determine how I am going to get away and find Celina. Sophie scares me and I don't doubt she would kill me if she felt threatened enough.

'We go now, boy.' She hands me another bowl of stew and I eat it gratefully. We stand mere inches apart and look into each other's eyes. She takes the bowl from my inert fingers, disappearing into the cave only to reappear seconds later with my coat.

'Come,' she says, and takes my hand; I pick up my bag and sling it over my shoulder.

'Where are we going?'

'Next place; must stay hidden, people looking for you, bad people and girl with red hair she looking as well.'

'Celina,' my voice questioning as she drags me along a grassy lane.

'You want to go back to her?' She stops turning her malevolent gaze on me.

'I... no, I was worried she got hurt back at the house,' I shrug. She takes my hands and ties them together with a cable tie. Looping rope around my waist she loops it around hers, so we are attached. 'You mine now,' she peers at me intently. Linking her fingers with mine.

'I won't run,'

'Don't trust boy,' her eyes narrow as she looks at me. She picks up the pace again. I look around. We are in a forest, not a wood as I first thought, and I can see trees in every direction soaring toward the sky. My foot catches in a root and I stumble.

'Come, boy.' she tugs my hand and starts running, zigzagging through the trees following a path only she can see. I am feeling tired and dizzy as sweat pours down my face.

'Please I can't run anymore, I say, bending down, my vision blurry as my head throbs, laboured breath rasping in my throat. She obviously knows nothing about how to treat a person with a head injury. My shirt clings to the sweat on my body and I feel disgusting, fantasising about showers and cool water.

'Hurry boy, nearly there. She takes my hand and pulls me along until we come to a clearing. 'Boy, you sit here.' She pulls me down. She is very physical. 'My name is Adam,' I explain, but I have a feeling she is still going to call me boy. She unties the rope from her waist.

'You stay here,' she grabs my ankles and produces another of her endless supply of cable ties. 'I hunt rabbit,' the grin she has on her face is one of confidence as she walks away from me. Stalking off, licking her finger, and sticking it in the air, circling back behind me until she disappears behind some bushes. Once she is gone. I wriggle about trying to get free. Eventually I lay back exhausted. I wriggle some more and manage to get my hands into my bag. My fingers brush my knife. Pulling it out I manoeuvre it so I can cut the tie around my ankles. Then I turn to cut the ones on my wrists this is tricky as I use a sawing action eventually it snaps. Putting my knife back in my bag I rub my sore wrists.

My thoughts turn to Sophie. She wants a boy, but do I want to be that boy? I glance around for her but can't see her. Moving into the trees I decide to wait for her to come back. I suspect I am in no position to escape her so maybe I can reason with her so we both gain a beneficial outcome.

My thoughts drift to her motives and what she wants me for. A baby, so that equals sex. Do I want that? Ultimately, no, not if I am just her captive? What if that isn't exactly what she wants? Could I love her? Could she love me? Could I achieve the freedom I desire? Well, it would appear not, my final rueful thought.

Taking out my bottle of water I gulp it down while I wait. I feel awful and it isn't just the headache. Celina was right and I suspect I am getting sick from the toxin. I know it is in everything, what I eat, the water I drink, that was how it had such a devastating effect, the reason everything I ate in the home was monitored and our blood tested. Should I find Celina! I don't particularly want to, but she would understand this sickness. What if I die? Oh, don't be an idiot; I will not die, well, not yet anyway. Sophie's sudden reappearance with a dead rabbit interrupts my musings.

'Look boy, I can look after you, we can be a family.' She looks around noticing the cable ties. From my hiding spot I see her frown and then shake her head. Turning she stalks around the place I was sat. With her back to me I creep up behind her and place my knife at her throat. A satisfied smirk on my face when she stiffens and drops her rabbit.

'I didn't run,' my voice menacing as I hold the knife tighter to her throat. 'I think it is time for a bit of negotiation,' I move around her, so we are facing each other my knife between us. Her face erupts into a huge smile as she appraises me.

'You will make fine babies,' she says with a confidence that bewilders me when I have the knife. Oh, who am I kidding she could have taken it from me quite easily.

'What if I don't want that?' I raise a brow as she scowls at me.

'Why wouldn't you,' she answers with a sulky pout. We sink to the floor crossed legged. Both watching the other.

'So, what is it you want from me?'

'I want a baby and be a family with boy,'

That's it?' I raise a brow at her nod. She is watching me warily and I can see how unsettled she is by this development. I doubt she thought this scenario would occur. A sadistic smile pulls at my lips.

'What does boy want?' She leans forward her large blue eyes fixed on me.

'Um not that,' I swallow. She pulls back unable to hide her disappointment. 'Look how about you help me, and I will try to give you a baby, but I don't know about the family bit,' She nods her head enthusiastically. 'I am looking for my brother. I wanted to see him once more before our status as Adams catches up with us,'

'I can help boy. I can help find brother and we can all be family,' she beams at me.

'That is very sweet, and I will consider your offer,' Climbing to my feet I hold out my hand to her. Pulling her up brings home how delicate and vulnerable she is. 'I need to be somewhere safe, somewhere secure for a bit. Do you understand,'

'Yes, I understand boy like me,' she beams at me taking my hand in her small one.

'How am I like you?'

'Boy is clean. Boy can make babies the natural way,' She picks up her dead rabbit and grabs my hand and before I know it, she has tied them again.

'Damn it Sophie, what did you do that for,' I grumble annoyed.

'Boy is treacherous,' she smirks as I scowl back. We walk through the woods in silence as she swings her dead rabbit. Which is weird and a bit creepy say nothing for disgusting.

CHAPTER 17

'Sophie, where is this?' We have been moving all day. Most of the villages we passed through had long ago been abandoned. The houses crumbling as vegetation reclaimed the land. I feel a kind of relief that we haven't seen another living soul. It is getting late, and I don't know where exactly we will spend the night. This is a worry nagging at the back of my mind as the dusk closes in.

Arriving at another derelict village, I climb over a crumbling wall and follow Sophie along a grass covered road. The church here is intact, which I find interesting stopping to admire it with its square Norman tower. Sophie grabs my hand and drags me away, causing me to stumble slightly.

'Church is treacherous boy you stay away,'

'Why, how?'

'It hides badness,' her odd answer and I want to question her more. Then I hear it the shuffle and cackle from the city. 'Common people,' I whisper.

'Yes boy,' she quickens her pace. She leads me to a house. I gaze up at it, taking in the grey stone it is built from. Even the roof is stone tiles covered in moss. Despite that, I can see it is sound, cared for and not collapsing.

'Just house halfway. Anyone can use it if you know where key is,' flashing a big grin as she pulls a loose stone and slips her fingers behind it. Pulling out a large iron key, she puts it in the lock on the door. I glance around. The derelict houses creep me out with the shapes thrown by the gathering dusk. A few houses like this one are intact though, the gardens tended and tidy, indicating people live here. Not that I get to see them. I briefly wonder where they are, what they do. Even when I was with Celina, I only saw a few people and that was mostly in the restaurant.

'Hurry boy,' Sophie pushes me inside and locks the door. I realise she is genuinely frightened.

'Sophie,' I watch her draw the curtains and light the lamps.

'Shush boy,' her hand to my mouth as she listens, I do the same as the door rattles. A cackle and the squeak of glass as something wet is wiped across it. My wide eyes glance at the window. We stand waiting until silence descends again. Sophie moves away from me.

'What was that?'

'The bad people,' Sophie shrugs as she puts her rabbit on the side.

Looking around I find myself in a basic kitchen. This room occupies the entire ground floor with a set of stone stairs leading to the upper floor tucked away in a corner. It is furnished with a small wooden table and four wooden chairs standing slightly off centre, with a faded sofa against the wall under the small window opposite the door we entered by. Dusty floral rugs cover the stone floor.

'Sophie, are we safe? Have they gone?'

'Yes, they gone. For now, we are safe in here.'

'Where did they go?'

'You ask a lot of questions.'

'Yeah, well, maybe I am fed up with being someone's prisoner and... and frightened all the time.' My voice is harsh, and I feel bad when she flinches. 'I need to know the dangers if I am going to stay safe,' my voice softer quieter.

'They go hunt.' I wait for her to elaborate, but annoyingly she doesn't.

'Hunt what?' I check the door is locked.

'Anything, us,' Sophie rummages in the cupboards.

She fills the Belfast sink before lighting a small. She has a pan of water on the little stove as she prepares dinner. The whole place is cosy and warm, very warm.

'Can you untie me please,' she huffs and marches over to me clearly annoyed. She grabs my hands jerking them up. Yep, she is annoyed. A tug and my hands are free. I rub my wrists red welts mark them. 'Thanks,' my smile saccharine sweet. She huffs and stalks back to the stove.

Shrugging out of my coat, pulling my sweater over my head hanging them on the back of a chair, she is watching me as she moves about. A blush stains my cheeks from her intense gaze. She turns away from me and I relax. My shoulders slump and I feel like I can breathe again. That was one intense look she gave me.

Sophie skins and guts her rabbit at the sink. Scrapping the chair against the stone tiles before lowering on to it, trying to look anywhere but at what Sophie is doing. I don't want to watch, but it is compelling in a disgusting sort of way, and I am eternally grateful that I didn't have to witness its demise. I hang my head and run my hand through my hair feeling the greasy grime. When did I last wash it? When did I last wash? These thoughts niggle what I assume is the start of a headache.

She chops the carcass of the rabbit and puts it in her pot with some vegetables she has in a bag; she produces a bottle of water and tips that in and then rummages about producing a stock cube, stirring the whole thing before putting the lid on. Sophie has been looking after herself for a long time. I watch as she takes some tins from her bag and places them in the cupboard.

'Have to replenish what we use. That's the rule,' She glances at me over her shoulder.

Sophie moves to sit with me. She doesn't say much, she just seems to like to be with me. She places her hand on my forehead, a frown creasing her brow; she moves her hand to my cheek.

'Boy, you are sick?'

'No just tired.' I reassure.

'Need to get you safe,' she peers at me intently and I find it disconcerting to say the least.

'Safe,' I can't help the mirthless laugh that escapes my lips. 'I am your prisoner. You are no better than the people you took me from,' my voice harsh.

'No, I am not. I will love boy and care for him properly,' she glares at me. 'Honour our agreement,' she nods as I give a snort of derision.

'I am not a bloody puppy. I am a person like you,' I am shouting now. surging to my feet I quiver with rage. I cast her a last look grabbing my clothing as I storm out the door slamming it shut as I take the stair two at a time needing distance. Finding a room with a dirty mattress on the floor I flop onto it and pull my knees up resting my head on them I let the tears flow. I know when she enters the room.

'Boy hungry?' Sophie places a bowl of stew on the floor and backs away. Her steps timid as she watches me. I stay still until she leaves the room. I crawl over and grab the bowl wolfing down the stew. It is surprisingly good.

I strip down to my T-shirt and boxers and crawl under the blankets; they don't smell very fresh, and I don't want to think about what else calls this place home. Still, it could be worse. It could be the tent. What am I doing I should leave? My final thought before I drift to sleep.

Sophie crawls in next to me and wraps around me. I let her even though my instinct is to pull away.

'Sorry boy,' she whispered her voice hitched on a sob and I hold her tight.

'I am sorry as well,' I whisper back.

CHAPTER 18

Stretching, I just lay still. I am alone. My thoughts drift to last night, the argument. She could have forced me; she could have done several things, but she didn't. Does that mean I should trust her? Wow, what is that smell? I am so hungry. What is wrong with me, life, and death situations and all I think about is food.

'Boy, you awake?'

'Yeah,' Sophie pushes the door open; her eyes scan me. A blush heats my cheeks as I pull my trousers on, her eyes on me the whole time.

'Tea,' she holds out a chipped mug to me.

'Thanks,' I take it, to find proper tea with milk. Wow didn't expect that. Briefly, I wonder where she got the milk from, of course, the farm we passed yesterday. Did she buy it or steal it? These thoughts trickle through as I sip the tea.

'Thanks Sophie,' I smile at her.

'Boy, been asleep a long time.' Have I! I look at my watch. It is past twelve, I still feel rubbish, but the headache has gone.

'Shall we start again,' I hold her gaze waiting for her answer.

'Yes,' she nods.

'You want a baby correct,'

'I ... I want a family with a boy, I want boy to love me,' She casts her gaze away from me. 'Then I want boy to give me a baby,'

'You can't force me to do that if I don't want to,'

'You are an Adam though,' her eyes meet mine, imploring.

'I am a person,'

'A boy person,'

'Yes, a boy person,' I chuckle.

'I am a girl person and boy person he can give me a baby and be family, yes,'

'Um, getting a head of yourself there,' I chuckle at her hopeful look. 'Lets just take this slow, yeah,'

'I like boy, he pretty and funny,' she jumps to her feet, an enormous smile on her face. 'Come boy, eat, then we leave,' she sort of skips out of the room, making me smile. Climbing to my feet, I grab my jumper, pulling it over my head. Picking up the mug, I follow her.

'I go now, you wait here,' Sophie gazes at me. She has doused the fire and packed the house up, making it look as if no one has been here. 'I check it safe,' she nods again and slips out the door. She hasn't tied me up so that's progress.

Eating the last of the stew, I mull over the conversation. I think I have successfully bargained with her. So, does that mean I can trust her? She will help me, not just impose her will. I like that. Moving to the sink, quickly washing the bowl and spoon, placing them on the side to dry, pulling on my coat that reminds me of Celina and I can't help wondering where she is. Should I have bargained with Celina? Except I have nothing she wanted. Celina had a match, and it wasn't me. Ellie didn't bargain either I muse. She made her intention pretty clear. Repeatedly through the night I smirk to myself.

Whereas Sophie wants a baby, and she wants me to give it to her. Does that make us equal? Peering outside, Sophie is nowhere to be seen. I lean against the door frame, fiddling with the strap to my bag. All of this I realise isn't getting me nearer to finding Aaron.

Sophie saunters up to me, an enormous smile on her face. Taking my hand, she leads me away from the small Hamlet. She has done her little trick again and my hands are tied. I sigh and hold them up with a raised brow.

'It looks better if boy is my prisoner,' she shrugs turning away I catch her smirk.

'Whatever,' my grumpy annoyed answer.

'Boy, ready!'

'Where are we going?' I enquire to be rewarded with one of her enigmatic smiles. Okay, so she isn't divulging that information.

'We go get a horse,' she states.

'Sophie, are we stealing a horse?' a frown mars my brow.

'Borrow boy, not steal,' Sophie pouts at me and it is all I can do not to laugh.

She takes my hands, pulling me along. 'You are mine now. I take care of you. When you know me better then you give me baby,' she mutters. She says it in a slightly scary way, sort of possessive and creepy.

'You wait here, boy,' she commands. She has only used my name once and I have kinda given up on trying to get her to use it. 'Don't run I will catch you,' she narrows her eyes as I roll mine. I watch as she scuttles away toward a barn. If someone had told me a few months ago, I would steal horses with strange girls. I would have laughed, but that is my reality right now and I kind of like it. Fidgeting enough to get my bag open so I can get my knife. My fingers wrap around its handle and I pull it out manoeuvring it to cut the ties.

In my estimation, I have been waiting three minutes when she reappears with a large bay horse. She seems in complete control as she rides it over to where I am crouched in the bush. I scramble to my feet and move over to Sophie and the horse. She grins at me, and I jump up behind her, wrapping my arms around her waist.

'Sophie, won't stealing a horse attract attention?'

'No, boy, should stay with me, he safer with me, boy should get rid of his map and forget girl with red hair, forget about finding brother, he probably dead, that would be better for boy,' she states and glances back at me.

'Sophie, when did you look at my map?' My body freezes as my cheeks flush, and I can't deny it. I am a bit annoyed by her. Obviously, she went through my things.

'When you were asleep for days, I wasn't sure you were going to wake up, ever, I found it in your bag.' Sophie answers she doesn't notice I am cross. She thought I would not wake up. That sort of puts it all into perspective.

'Sophie, do you know what UHF is?'

'Yes, they are as bad as Gen-Corp, they will take boy and hurt him.'

'Why would they hurt me?'

'You annoy me with your questions boy, everything broken now, even Adams broken.' she pauses and gazes at me, making me feel uncomfortable. 'They hunt you, they rarely bother, you are different, you aren't broken, you like me, you can resist the toxin, that why you are sick, you are fighting the toxin, purging it from your system. Boy, will be clean, boy, will make babies.'

'What do you mean, like you, when you say toxin, do you mean the contraceptive?'

'Yes boy, that's why you are sick, but soon you will adjust

and be well again.' The countryside slips away as I mull over everything. Sophie urges the horse on faster. I wrap my arms around her waist my cheek against her back letting my eyes slip closed. My head still aches. The light aggravates it.

'How do you know all that?' I mutter.

'Information is there if you know where to look, had to know how to care for Adam if I was going to have one of my own.' Well put like that, she makes it sound like she is gaining a pet! In a way, I suppose she is, and that really bothers me. The other thing that bothers me is I know she is lying, and I can't think why? Out here where would she get that information? There is no access to technology out here. Let it go Adam I think to myself.

'Where are we going?'

'Commune.'

'Oh,' I have no idea what that is. Her posture is ridged so I guess I am annoying her now, so shut up. 'Is that where you live?' okay so I couldn't contain my curiosity. Besides I don't fully trust her.

'Yes boy, it is a good place.'

CHAPTER 19

Someone is slapping my face.

'Boy wake up,' Sophies voice penetrates through the fog in my head. I open my eyes to find I am in front of Sophie slumped against her. One of her arms has me anchored in place. Rubbing my hand down my face as I blink awake. I glance around noticing we are on a road that snakes between overgrown hedges alive with birds and rabbits.

Sophie eventually turns off the road and follows a green path through a meadow and into a wood.

'Sophie, I can hear voices,' looking through the trees, I can't make out any figures.

'Yes boy, nearly there.' Sophie pulls the horse to a stop and jumps down. Gazing around, I hold the reins to the horse tighter than I should. I feel as if I am being watched. I slide off and slump down as my legs tremble from being on the horse for so long.

Putting her hands to her mouth, she hoots like an owl, making me startle slightly. Sophie glares at me and then takes my hand as all around us I hear owl hoots in reply. Slowly, out of the trees and gloom, people appear.

'Don't feel good can't run,' I mumble out.

'We safe now, boy,' Sophie says and takes my hand as she walks through the woods. I walk to her side, not understanding where we are. I stop when I see figures appear around us emerging from the trees.

'They are friends,' Sophie smiles and I swallow nervously, not really convinced. One of them walks up to Sophie and hugs her. They part and the woman looks me over. I say woman loosely. I use that description because I know I am possibly the only male on this continent. Okay, that might be a slight exaggeration, but I am unlikely to meet a proper male soon. On reflection, I am unlikely to meet another Adam either. Pulling my hood up to cover my face, I decide hiding the fact I am male might be a good idea.

The woman is ugly. That's the only way I can describe her. She looks as if she has run into a wall repeatedly. Her nose is kind of flat and there are many scars criss-crossing her face. In all fairness, she may have been pretty once, but hard to visualise at this precise moment and actually it's quite refreshing. I have spent far too much time with beautiful people, well Adams mainly, since they breed us to be physically perfect. An imperfection is almost a shock.

'This mate, this your boy?' The woman looks me over. Her gaze rests on me and a slow smile crosses her face, revealing broken yellow teeth. So much for disguising the fact I am male. Sophie just blabs it out. I tense up and try to see if there is an escape route should this turn nasty.

'Yes, this boy is mine,' Sophie answers and holds my hand tighter.

'You breed?'

'Yes,' Sophie answers and I have a feeling this is a pivotal moment in our survival.

'You come with us, you safe now,' the woman nods at us and turns and joins the rest of her group. She speaks to them in a rapid language I don't understand. The group look over at us and then back at her before nodding in unison. I'm not sure about this.

'Sophie, who are these people?' My voice low, as I look at Sophie, searching her face.

'They, my people,' Sophie nods, indicating the discussion is over. 'Boy, worry too much, boy sick.' She announces.

'Yeah, boy sick,' I acknowledge.

We walk for about twenty minutes, by my estimation, from what I can see we are walking through farmland, and I wonder if it belongs to this group of people. This is so different from when I was on the run with Celina. It is open and I can see miles of flat countryside. I smell the wood smoke before I see the village and I am so glad I can see houses. For a minute I had visions of huts, not that I mind huts, but I really prefer houses. Over thinking again, no wonder I have a headache again.

'Boy, you very pale, you, okay?' Sophie peers at me.

I smile at her and kiss her cheek. 'Headache back,' I mutter, blinking my eyes slowly in an effort to stay awake, making her chuckle. I feel lightheaded. I grab Sophie, as I feel dizzy.

'You, idiotic boy, you need bed, you very sick,' Sophie pulls me forward. We walk through a wood and enter a clearing with a stream running through it. On the far side, a small cluster of houses surround a church. The place is busy with people, more people than I have ever seen in one place since being out here. No one takes any notice of us, or me even. As people go about their business, I stop and just look around, completely taken aback. This was not what I was expecting.

'Dad says you can put the horse in his stable, Miss Sophie,' the child stands and looks at us. I reel at this sentence as I swear, she said dad, as in a man. 'You found a mate then?'

The girl surveys me. 'Small for an Adam, is he legal age?' She cocks her head to one side and regards me. Wow, she is forward for a child. Apart from other Adams I have never met a child. She completely fascinates me.

'How old are you?'

'Ten, how old are you?'

'Eighteen I think,'

'You don't know?' she cocks her head to one side.

'I don't know the month,' I confess.

'April,'

'Eighteen then,'

'Polly, that is kind of your dad, yes I found a boy.' What the hell, she said dad.

'What is this place?' Turning I gaze around at the small hamlet with its people.

'Come, boy.' Sophie tugs on my hand.

'Are there men and more children here?' The shock makes me stutter, turning my gaze to Sophie.

'Yes boy, of course there are.' Sophie shakes her head and looks at me like I am stupid. 'Boy is tired, need to sleep,' she stands altogether too close, before turning and opening the gate leading toward the house.

I don't know what I was expecting, but this house is clean and modern inside. Sophie leads me through the downstairs that comprised two rooms, a kitchen diner, and a small living room, and up the open stairs to a bedroom. I put my bag on a chair in the bedroom and then shuffle to the bathroom, stripping; I have a much-needed shower.

I stand in the shower, leaning my palms against the tiles. Just letting the water run over me, seeing the slight brown colour as I wash the blood out of my hair. I put my fingers to my head and flinch as I touch the raised lump on the back of my head, wrapping a towel around my waist, before walking back to the bedroom. Only to find my clothes have gone and been replaced by some pyjamas. I put them on and crawl into bed, not caring that I haven't eaten or that it is still light outside. The bed is so soft and smells of flowers. Falling asleep is much easier than I had expected. Waking as someone wipes my face with a cool cloth, my body shakes and sweats, as I mumble incoherently, the temperature burning me up.

'Boy, he very sick?'

'Yes, Sophie, just keep bathing him, the fever should break in a day or two.'

'He doesn't like me,'

'Oh Sophie, give him time,'

'He is Echo, whether he likes you or not won't matter. You know how this works,'

'Yes, Elder Elaine, but what if he despises me,'

'He won't sweetheart the bond will snap into place,' Silence shrouds the room as I feel hands touching, putting dry pyjamas on me, before I sleep again.

Light through a gap in the curtains wakes me. Reaching for my watch, to see the time. I don't know how long I have been here. One day, maybe two, it is mid-afternoon now. Closing my eyes again, I note that the headache has gone, and I don't feel as feverish as I did. I don't want to get up yet, so I just lay in the bed snug, warm, safe, reluctant to move. I wake to the dark and quiet. Another day missed. Sophie has her arm around my waist, her head by my shoulder, sound asleep. I kiss her hair and drift back to sleep.

When I wake, she is gone, and her pillow is cold. I can see faint daylight through the curtain. I shuffle out of bed and find my clothes washed and clean, folded neatly on a chair. I get dressed and meander downstairs. I can hear Sophie and follow the sound of her voice to the kitchen. She is not alone, and they are talking about me, and I know I shouldn't, but I listen concealed by the door.

'Sophie, he isn't a retiree, he should still be in a home with a Mother.'

'Boy, he is mine. I watched him run,' Sophie states.

'You want to keep him; you know if you get caught, they will shoot you on sight.'

'Have to find me first,'

'Oh, Sophie, what am I going to do with you?' Hearing a fondness in the stranger's voice.

'Boy so frightened, let me keep him,' Sophie is begging, and I smile.

'He is not some puppy you can rescue; remember that one a few summers ago that bit you? That's what he will do,' I hear Sophie sigh.

'Boy said that he shouted was very angry,' I can hear the sulkiness in her voice and smirk. Glad she didn't like me shouting.

'You said he doesn't like you explain? Was it because you compared him to a pet?' Sophie nods.

'He ran away so I tied him up,' Sophie whispers.

'Ah, okay, and now how does he feel about that?'

'He, I don't know. He says he wants to find his brother, but he said he would give me a baby if I helped him. Be a family,' Sophie is pleading, and I feel bad.

'He is like me, we are the same, you saw how sick he was.'

'Sophie, he should not be free. It doesn't matter what he is. He should be in a home.'

'But he is, he mine now, boy not going back, they will euthanise him,' she is almost shouting.

'Sophie, think about this, he is underage, has no name, there has to be a reason for that. The elders could find no records for him someone has hidden him for a reason. His number didn't match on the data base.'

'He won't be on there he isn't retired,' Sophie grumbles.

'He should still be on it Sophie. Sophie, think. People are

looking for him, like they looked for you. They will not euthanise him, they want him back, for something else.'

'No, he is mine not for something else. I was sent to his home to collect samples and talk to his Mother. I was to meet him, get to know him. I never ask for anything and I wanted this one thing,' She is on her feet shouting and tears are wobbling her voice.

'Sophie calm down, sweety,'

'He ran and then Celina found him. It has taken months to track him down. He belongs to us, to me,' Sophies voice is eloquent with her anger. Whoa hang on she was at my home watched me run. She sinks back down her posture crumpled in defeat.

'Is that so, I need to contact your mother,'

'No, no please don't. Mother wants him for Florence not me. Florence doesn't want him, I do,' Sophie is begging. Her voice is frightened. Who is Florence?

'Hm, not a good match for Florence to delicate.'

'I failed and she is punishing me,' Sophie sniffles.

'No sweetie, let me talk to her. In the meantime, he can stay with you. If he leaves you let him go. It is too dangerous to keep chasing him understand,'

'He will stay, he promised,' Sophie grumbles.

'Sophie, just be careful, that's all I'm saying. I will speak to the other elders, and we will give him a trial period. If he fits in and no one comes looking, you can keep him, but if people come looking, you give him back. And Sophie I will be speaking to your mother.'

'Yes, Elder Elaine, understand?' Sophie reply's her voice sulky.

'Oh, and Sophie, you must explain about Echo's give him the choice,'

'But he won't do it if I tell him,'

'Sophie,'

'Yes, Elder Elain,' Sophie huffs out the last sentence clearly annoyed.

That was all I needed to hear. Edging away from the door I take the stairs two at a time. Entering the room, I had been put in I retrieved my bag and my coat. Opening the window, I looked down. Climbing out, I carefully lowered myself down and dropped the last few feet. With a final look at the house, I circled around to the back and cross to the wood surrounding the cluster of houses. The same wood I had walked through with Sophie.

Not my finest plan but I was damned if I was just going to give up my freedom to become some sort of prize breeding stallion. I sneak through the wood pleased with myself as I seem to have escaped undetected.

The first indication I am not alone is the snapping of a twig. I freeze and peer around before stepping behind an impressive oak tree. Reaching into my bag I pull my knife out. I lean slightly around the tree to try and catch a glimpse of whoever is following me.

'Sophie,' I mutter as a knife is pressed to my throat from behind. Her distinctive scent invades my nostrils. A mix of summer rain on wet earth and roses.

'You ran boy,' she moves in front of me the knife still at my throat as I am pinned to the tree.

'Well, yeah,' I shrug a smirk on my face as I stand watching her. My posture one of defiance.

'Why?' Her expression shows her hurt and betrayal at my behaviour. I sigh and look up at her. 'You promised,' her voice is filled with disappointment and a shimmer of tears glisten in her eyes.

'I refuse to swap one prison for another. You are just offering nothing more than I escaped from. So why would I stay?' I have manoeuvred my knife into her side and press it so she can feel it. A slow smile pulls at her lips. Her eyes hold my gaze and then drift to my lips. The tension crackles between us. 'I don't even like you,' I whisper in her ear. She trembles and then pulls herself up pushing back her shoulders. A wicked gleam in her eyes.

'I will show boy why he should stay,' she declares before her mouth crashes against mine. I have never been kissed like this. It is urgent, demanding, nothing gentle about it. I feel my arousal as I realise, I like it.

I spin her around and push her against the tree taking her hands and raising them above her head. She doesn't resist as my tongue plunders her mouth. The knives clatter to the ground.

'Is this what you want?' I hoist her skirt up around her waist her fingers scramble at my zip. I wrap her legs around my waist with a surge of my hips she cries out.

'Yes, I want you,' she pants out. Her hands fist in my hair. The sharp pain of my scalp adds to my pleasure. I feel whole, complete. That part that has always been missing is filled. I can feel her emotions and I suspect she can feel mine as we seem to connect. This is not gentle or sweet it is rough and animalistic.

A crow screeches above us as we both cry out together. Sinking to the forest floor. We lay panting our sweat mingles with our breath as we both try to drag precious air into our lungs.

'What was that?' I finally pant out because that was nothing like I experienced with Ellie. Anger fills me as I glare at her. While at the same time I want her again. I think I hate her but at the same time want her again. What is wrong with me? I pull her against me kissing her roughly.

'We are the same boy. Perfectly matched for each other. You are mine and I am yours. Made to cure this broken world. Dr Echo made sure when we found each other we would breed. Changing our DNA leaving nothing to chance.' She says as she straddles my hips, and we go again.

I scramble away from her once we finish. Pulling up my trousers I grab my shirt from the ground. She adjusts her clothes as I do the same. She stands and holds her hand out to me. I glare at it and stomp past her doing up my coat, straightening my bag over my head.

'No more running boy,' she grabs my arm pulling me around to face her.

'What are we?' I narrow my eyes at her.

'I am Echo, a princess of Tribe and you are mine. You are Echo boy,'

'What the hell does that mean,' I growl.

'It means no more running,'

'No more running,' I smirk. 'How will you stop me?' I raise a brow.

'You are mine.' Her sultry voice whispers in my ear. I pull her to me and plunder her mouth as she tries to dominate me. I want her again what the hell.

'When we get back you are going to tell me everything. Do you understand,' I fix her with my sternest glare because somehow, I think Aaron is mixed up in this. Something I overheard a long time ago.

CHAPTER 20

Yanking the door open I step inside glaring at Sophie as she strolls in smirking at me. Like she knows a secret, her whole stance one of superiority and I hate it. I hate that I want her again that she has this power over me. I grab her arm and the minute I touch her I want to take her on the floor, the table, against the wall. With an angry kick the door slams shut.

'What have you done to me Sophie,' I growl at her as I pin her to the door I have just slammed shut.

'You are an Echo boy, and I am an Echo girl. When we find each other, we are compelled to reproduce,' she gasps as I crush her mouth with mine.

'This feeling how long will it last,' her hands are at my waist band. Mine are on her breasts.

'Until I get pregnant,' she lets out a moan and arches her back rubbing against me. 'Being together has triggered our bodies need to reproduce,' she pants ripping my shirt as I kick my jeans off.

'How did you know I was a... Echo?' I spin her around pushing her skirt up I take her again.

'My Mother sent me to observe you. I was to meet with your Mother. I was meant to collect a blood sample and a sperm sample to take back. Meet you, get to know you. Then wait for you to come of age as the agreement dictates. Only you ran. You are good at running boy,' she groans her hands flat against the door as she pushes back onto me matching my frenetic pace. 'You like the other boys were hidden in plain sight to keep you safe. You and your brother belong to us. He is matched to my sister,'

Where is my brother?' My movements sloppy.

'He is safe, in a facility belonging to Gen-Corp in France' she moans out as her body shudders against mine. Sinking to the floor. 'When he comes of age my sister will collect him,'

'How many boys are there like me?' I pull my jeans back on my shirt ruined.

'About half a dozen. My Mother has a deal with Gen-Corp. Your brother was always ours you were a surprise no one knew what to do with. So, a deal was struck making you ours as well. You are meant for my sister Florence, but she doesn't want you. So, I asked if I could meet you and mother said yes,' she scrambles to her feet moving away from me.

'You were going to take me though weren't you,' this realisation slams into me. Standing I run a hand through my hair. 'You were going to take me before you left, despite my age,'

'Yes, because Mother struck a deal with Gillian and Gen-Corp. To sell you back to them until you were twenty,' I am shocked at this bit of information.

'But I had seen you then. Met with Emma,' she can't meet my gaze. 'Florence isn't right for you, she... she is to... brutal. Gillian she would have ruined you,' I raise a brow at this answer. 'It wasn't meant to be like this, and I am sorry truly I am,' a sob catches in her throat as she runs from the kitchen toward the stairs. I sink on to a chair not sure what to think.

When I can think coherently. My brain constantly shifting to her and carnal thoughts. Pulling my coat on I have to get out of this house. While at the same time I know I can't leave. Damn her. I find myself sat on the bench overlooking the river. A pretty stone bridge linking the village to the road. I can see the silver haze of the disused solar farm glinting in the sunshine. Dropping my head into my hands I start to cry.

'Adam?' the voice is tentative as if frightened I will bolt. Wiping my face, I look up. It's the woman who was talking to Sophie. 'May I join you?' I nod not trusting myself to speak. We sit in silence. 'She found you then,'

'Yes,'

'Why did you run?'

'Being here is just swapping one prison for another. This is more attractive than the home, but it is still the same. I still belong to a stranger with no control over my life or what I want,'

'You can leave, I can make sure no one stops you,' I turn to look at her.

'You would do that for me! Someone you hardly know, knowing it will hurt Sophie?'

'Yes,'

'Why?' I narrow my eyes as I study her.

'We are not Gen-Corp we don't hold hostages. If you don't want to be here, we will not force you,'

'And Sophie what is your obligation to her?'

'None, she belongs to the Royal house of Tribe. The youngest daughter of the current queen. She will return to them with her baby,'

'Why is she here?' I frown trying to piece together all my information.

'She like you doesn't want the life given to her. She broke the rules. A baby is her route to forgiveness. You and

Sophie are more alike than you think,' she takes my hands. 'Adam, you ran away because you wanted something else other than the situation you were in. I can't presume to know what it is you want but if you stay you will have a family, a home and if you want a fulfilled life,' she lets go of my hands and climbs to her feet. 'It is up to you to find that fulfilment,' I watch her walk away. My gaze drifts to the solar farm.

SOPHIE GLANCES up at me as she rolls out her pastry. Pulling out a chair I sink onto it reaching out I snag a warm biscuit. She smacks my hand and raises a brow. I smirk and shove the warm biscuit in my mouth.

'Boy,' she glares at me.

'Girl,' I retaliate. Her bottom lip wobbles.

'Oh, for goodness' sake don't cry,' pushing to my feet I move to her and pull her into my arms. 'Sorry,' I kiss her.

'Why are you still here?' she looks up at me.

'Where else would I be. I know where my brother is and he is safe. If you are pregnant, I want to be involved. So, tell me where else would I be?'

'You don't want me though,' her voice wobbles.

'I hardly know you and I want that to change,'

'You do?'

'Yes, I want to get to know you.'

'I want to get to know you as well boy,' her face lights up with a smile.

'Good, so I am going to fix the solar farm to run the village and get to know you better so we can be family.' I open the manual and start reading. She watches me for a bit before going back to her baking. I am hoping the pie she is making the top for is going to be supper.

My attention is now focused on the solar farm. I know it

doesn't work and I want to know why. Could I get it to work and run the village and farm? It might be the purpose I seek.

The next morning, I climb over the gate that leads into the field where the solar panels are and walk between them. I make a quick inspection of some panels. Although old and grimy, they don't appear to be damaged. I then take the time to look between the panels themselves and can see that the insulated pipes running between them are not damaged. I follow it to the end where the pipes from each row of panels links together and heads towards the generator building.

Following the pipe, I can see that it is also undamaged as it heads into the generator building. I sheepishly look around to see if anyone is about before peering through the grimy window into the building. It appears deserted; I try the door handle to find that is locked, confirming that it must be empty. I wander around the building to find some old wooden boxes that I might be able to climb on to get in one window. After rooting around some more, I find some old metal tools lying around.

I grab a pry bar and push the wooden box next to one window before using the pry bar to force one of the window shutters open. After a brief struggle, I worm myself through the window and fall gracelessly to the ground of the generator building.

The turbine is identifiable as a large cylinder depressed into the ground. The water from the solar farm is passed from the insulated pipe through the generator before returning to the solar panels. I can see from a readout that the generator is in fact producing 5% power and that water is flowing sluggishly through the system.

So why are the lights still off? I follow the electrical cables coming from the generator to a large breaker switch, set to off. Bingo! I exclaim. I bet if I flip that there will be power. I grab the switch and push it up into the on position...

Nothing happens. I flick the light switch by the door. Still nothing and none of the diodes on the control panel have lit up either. Perplexed, I glare angrily at the dead control panel. I return to the breaker and continue following the wires. They lead into a separate room where they connect to a large battery, which, judging by the burn marks and rust I surmise, is totally busted. I return to the breaker and set it back to off, so I don't electrocute myself accidentally. I then return to the broken battery to figure out how to fix it.

After some considerable effort, I manage to remove the broken battery from its dock and push it into the corner out of the way. I then set about searching around for a replacement. I remember the wooden boxes outside and wonder if any of them have a spare battery in. I head out and walk to a storage shed, forcing the door I peer inside. After rooting around for a bit, I find a wooden box with the same company name on the side as the broken battery. I pry the box open and am greeted with success, a brand-new shiny battery. How am I going to lift it on my own?

I search around some more and finally find a wheeled trolley. After a struggle, I get the battery onto the trolley and wheel it back to the generator building. With considerable effort I get it installed and head back to the breaker switch. After a brief hesitation, I flick the switch…again nothing happens.

Defeated I flop into the office chair next to the main console and stare grumpily off into space. When I notice a slight glow coming from the old filament bulb hanging in the middle of the room, I look at the control panel and see that the green diodes are beginning to light up faintly. It's working! I fixed it! I yell with excitement and set off sprinting from the generator building and along the road to the village.

I follow the overhead electrical cables all the way and can see that they are all still connected. They fan out and connect to the houses. Rushing to mine I burst through the door startling Sophie as she prepares dinner. She watches perplexed as I rummage about in the cupboard under the stairs finding the fuse and power box. Studying this I realise I need to disconnect the generator.

'Boy, what are you doing?' Sophie asks baffled by my behaviour.

'I think I have the solar farm working,' rushing out the door again hurrying around the back to the generator. Gazing up at the cable I follow it until I can see where the generator is crudely connected to the power line for the house. Switching off the generator the house is plunged into darkness.

'Adam!' Sophie shouts. Her voice clearly annoyed she used my name. Running back inside I squeeze back into the cupboard under the stairs. Finding the switch, I push it on. Waiting as the house comes to life again. The lights come back on barely, the power plant is working and providing power but not nearly enough. I would have to go back and try and find a way of boosting the output. I reconnect the generator and the house lights up once again.

'It works,' I cheer grabbing Sophie I dance around the kitchen with her making her giggle.

Chapter Twenty One

Today I start my new job officially. I obtained permission to look at the solar farm and find out why it doesn't work. I need to clean the panels and get it working. I want it efficient enough to run the village. Getting the diesel is hard it makes us vulnerable, and it would be better if we didn't rely on it. I found the maintenance manuals and have read them repeatedly.

I get dressed making as little sound as possible. Strolling through the sleeping village I am surprised when I come across a boy sat on the bench by the pond. As I draw near, I realise he is crying. I hesitate and then approach him.

'Hello,' he jerks his head up startled by my presence. Wiping his face on his sleeve he looks me over.

'Hello,' his voice wobbles. He is stunning. Like Mathew, he is perfect in every way. From his black hair, green eyes. His face is beautiful. A true Adam. 'You, you are a male,' he stutters out.

'Hi, I'm Adam,' I hold my hand out to him. He hesitates and then shakes it. 'Are you okay?'

'Jake,' he takes in a breath and wipes his face. 'Yes, I mean no, I,' he bites his lip, and I can see his eyes are watery again.

'Hey, come on don't cry,' I sit next to him and take his hand.

'I can't do what she wants... she looks at me and I can see the disappointment. But I just can't,' he lets out a sob and the tears spill over.

'Hey, come on, it will be alright you just have to take it slow,' oh yeah great advice like you and Sophie so did that. I think to myself, remembering the woods and the week that followed but that was not normal. That was something else and he is an Adam not a stupid Echo.

'Where are you going?' He stutters out wiping his face.

'To the solar farm. I am trying to get it working,' I show him the manual.

'Do you want some help?' He wipes his face with his sleeve.

'Sure,' He pushes to his feet.

'Thank you,' he mumbles out and drops into step with me.

We spend the morning cleaning the actual panels and looking them over for broken bits. Checking they are still connected. The store shed I found the battery in is full of equipment. Jake consults the instruction manual and has been reading bits of it. It seems he needed a distraction as well. I have my first real friend and that gives me a thrill. I miss Matthew and it would be nice to talk to another male. Not that he talks much. Only to ask a question about the task.

'Right let's see if it works,' I wipe my hands on my trousers as nerves get to me. What if I can't get it to work? No, it will work.

'How are you going to do that,' Jake wipes his hands on a bit of rag.

'Well let's connect your house to it and see,'

'Okay,' He mumbles. He hasn't said much over the morning, and I haven't pressured him. I do know he belongs to Gemma and only arrived here last month. The sickness kept him from being introduced to everyone. 'You won't burn it down?' His questioning gaze makes me laugh.

'I hope not,' I glance at him as we walk to the village. He raises a brow, and a smile pulls at his lips. 'Gemma would be very cross,' I snigger, and he gives a chuckle as I nudge his shoulder.

'Yes, she would,' his voice sombre as the mirth melts away.

'Hi Gemma,' I call out the greeting as I push the door open. Gemma is a petit little thing, crazy hair, and eyes that twinkle with mischief. She and Sophie are friendly, so I am acquainted with her.

'Hi Adam,' she looks past me to Jake and bites her lip. 'Um its laundry day so I will be out your way. Have you come to connect us to the solar farm?' She picks up her basket of laundry. I had to ask the Elders if it was okay for me to fix it so the entire village know what I do most days.

'Yeah, hopefully,' She shuffles past us out the door. Jake slumps onto a chair and burst into tears again. His head in his hands as his shoulders shake with his sobs.

'Hey, come on,' I sooth.

'I can't do it… and…and I want to but…'

'Jake, you have to give it time. No one expects you to okay,' I kneel in front of him. 'You have to get to know her first and then progress from there,'

'She won't send me away?'

'Goodness no,' climbing to my feet I pass him my hanky and fetch him a glass of water.

'Is that what you and Sophie did?' his gaze fixed on me. I laugh.

'Something like that. Sophie and I arrived here together. She … um rescued me when I ran into a bit of trouble,'

'So, she didn't get you from a home?'

'No, I was with the united Human Federation. Being escorted to Ireland.'

'Wow really! Don't you want to go back to them?' His eyes are wide as he appraises me. 'How old are you?' His brow pulls into a frown.

'Um eighteen. No, not particularly,' I confess.

'How can you be eighteen? Why don't you want to go with them?'

'That was a lot of questions,' I chuckle while thinking how to answer. Because they were good questions. 'I didn't fancy what they had in mind for my future. I ran away to avoid other people's plans for me,' I answer although that was lame and now, I am not sure what my future will be if we have made a baby. 'Sophie and I are Echo's so its all much more complicated,' giving him a shrug and smile.

'You ran away?' His eyes widen in awe or surprise or both I am not sure.

'Yeah, crazy,'

'Amazing more like. So, you like it here with Sophie?'

'Yes, Sophie… is challenging,' I know I have a huge grin on my face. 'It wasn't always like that. Sophie and I didn't immediately hit it off,' my answer candid.

'You are very lucky,' he answers with a snivel.

'Come on you will get there. Me and Sophie we had to work at being friends,'

'Thank you,' he mutters and sips the water. He watches me as I switch the house over from the generator to the solar farm. Eventually it will run the entire village.

'See you tomorrow, Jake,' I say cheerfully as I let myself out. I amble back to the solar field I have some reading I need to catch up on.

Pulling my flask and lunch box from my bag eating while I read. Time slips by unnoticed by me, so absorbed in the manual. My head only lifts as I hear my name being called, only now noticing it is getting dark. Collecting my things and putting the manual in my bag, I slowly rise to my feet, stretching my cramped muscles. Pushing the door open, I am amazed to find people calling my name.

'Found him!' someone shouts.

'I am here,' jogging to the village amazed as Sophie comes flying across the bridge at a dead run, almost knocking me down. 'Hey what's going on?'

'I thought I lost you.' Her hands cup my face as her lips find mine. The kiss soft and urgent, desperate even. 'You didn't come home for dinner and when I talked to Jake, he said he hadn't seen you all afternoon.'

'How could you lose me?' I chuckle. 'I hope you were gentle with Jake he is very emotionally delicate,' I tease her as she looks at me like I am an idiot.

'There are bad people in the area. I thought... you are very valuable,' her gaze trained on my face, fear clear in her eyes.

'I am safe, see. No one has taken me,' amazement paints my tone. Leaning in I kiss her. Reassuring her that I am okay. 'I am here quite safe,' I mumble between kisses.

'I release you,' she hangs her head, 'I know you aren't happy here, so I release you from the promise,' Stepping back she initiates the distance between us.

'Hey, no I am happy. I like being with you,' placing my finger under her chin so she looks me in the eye. Leaning in I kiss her beautiful mouth as her body moulds to mine. 'You won me over,' our foreheads press together. 'These last week's fixing the solar farm I have a purpose of my choosing. I had a chat with Elder Elaine,' I confess a sheepish smile on my face.

'Really what did she say to boy,' Sophie frowns.

'She said I could leave if I wanted,'

'Oh,' her face crumples into distress again.

'But she also reminded me I have a home here and family,'

'You want family with me? You will make baby with me?' her big eyes search my face for any sign of deception.

'Yes, I want that. All of that with you,' I kiss her again. The baby bit I think is a moot point after that week.

My eyes track the moon as clouds pass in front of it. Turning, I gaze at Sophie asleep next to me. Dinner was forgotten as we spent our time reaffirming the bond. If she is pregnant that makes her as valuable as me if not more so. I pull her close, my arm around her. She turns toward me; her lips find mine.

'Boy,' she mutters in her sleep, her limbs wrapped around me. At last I have a purpose and someone to love that loves me back.

CHAPTER 21

Sat in the office my eyes flick to the board to check the output. I read the manual about maintaining the solar farm. I have almost got the solar farm running all the houses now. Only looking up when I hear the handle to the front door rattle and then open. Glancing up, hoping it is Sophie I see two people walk past the window.

Instinct has me rolling on to the floor and out of view. Crawling to the side door, carefully opening it, I peer outside to see the back of a group of women. They are a scary bunch, all dressed in black with leather jackets 'Dread Riders' painted on the back. Pulling my boots on and grabbing my bag I sit concealed. Why are they here?

'Look at this its working,' two have stepped into the office.

'Helena said he is a clever little…'

'Yeah, I heard rumours they had males here that knew stuff,'

'Males don't need to know stuff they just need to know how to pleasure a woman,' they cackle with laughter as they move away.

'Well, the one we want doesn't appear to be here,'

'He ain't here. Helena will be mad.'

'They might be hiding him.'

'Well, of course they are. Did you see the girl at the church? I bet my bike she is an Echo.'

'That Elder Elaine she is a crafty old witch. I bet they have the Echo boy hidden someplace.'

'They have a couple of nice Adams here as well. They would fetch a good price,'

'Best search this place then,'

'Gen-Corp are here. Did you see all that security?' They turn to the door, and I breathe a sigh of relief when they leave. I grab my stuff and make my way to the back door. Peering outside I slip into the store shed and then out behind the huts. Climbing the church-yard wall, I make my way through the headstones. Dread riders are sat in groups laughing and talking, blocking the way. I have been gone longer than I thought, and the shadows are lengthening.

Sitting concealed behind a tombstone, I try to decide what to do as shouting drifts around me. Looking up, I see the girls talking and then disperse into the woods. With relief I go to get up, only to have a hand cover my mouth and push me down.

'Don't move if they catch us, they will shoot us,' her soft lilting voice whispers in my ear her body quivers with fright.

'Sophie,' I breathe out and she replaces her hand with her mouth. My body reacts immediately. Pulling back, she gazes at me worry in her eyes.

'You must run boy, or they will take you. We don't have papers for you,' her eyes dart around the graveyard before settling on me again. 'Go to the forest and hide I will find you when it is safe,'

'No Sophie, they will hurt you,' I argue.

'I am safe boy...' climbing to her feet she pulls me up. 'Go now, go to the farm the other side of the wood,' with one last fleeting kiss I move in the direction of the forest. Gazing back once to see her stroll into the village.

I can't see anyone. As I slip into the trees following the path for a bit. I move from the path and head to a place Sophie, and I go to for picnics it is near a bend in the river.

'Oi, you stop,' I turn to see a group of women heading toward me.

'It's him,' one shouts, and I break into a run. I make it into the trees as shots ring out. Darting around vegetation I can hear their booted feet behind me. More shots as a bullet embeds in a tree near me. Splinters showering the space around me. I run again dodging around the trees zigzagging. A thump and pain in my side has me stumbling. I manage to stay on my feet. I can hear them crashing through the undergrowth. I slip and tumble down a bank rolling end over end until I come to a stop. My head hits something hard. Stars spin in front of my eyes blinking to try and clear them, I can feel warm wet of blood. I shut my eyes laying still trying to gather myself if I pass out, I am frightened I won't wake up again... ever.

'Up you get,' arms wrap around me hauling me to my feet A groan leaves my lips as I clutch my side feeling the warm wet of blood trickling over my fingers. 'Let me see that,' her voice soft as she pulls my fingers away. She lifts my jumper and undoes my shirt. I glance up at her. Gen-Corp security judging by her uniform.

'Can you walk?'

'Yes, think so,' I wince.

'Right let's move it isn't safe here,' she wraps her arm around me lending support.

I can hear the whine of jet engines steadily getting closer. My body trembles first with fatigue from the constant pain and then with fear. We have been running for a few minutes when the gunfire really starts and bullets whizz past us. I stumble from the force of something brushing my arm and I feel a stinging sensation and a flare of pain. I almost drop to the ground as a she pulls me up.

'You okay Adam?' her voice in my ear. As I stumble again the blood loss taking its toll.

The gun fire seems to get heavier as one of those black jets comes into view above us. I feel a hand on my arm, and I am pulled roughly sideways through a hedge. I feel the branches scratch at my face and hands as a group of soldiers intercept us on the other side. These aren't Gen-Corp soldiers, their uniform is different. I see a soldier run forward with a rocket launcher perched on her shoulder; I hear the hiss as the rocket shoots and hear the bang as it hits its target. A flare of intense light illuminates the battle.

I lie sprawling to the ground, squinting in the dawn light as another great black jet hovers into view. It is sleek and smooth, with some sort of cannon mounted at the front. I swallow in terror as I see the cannon is trained intently on me. It hovers motionless above me as six sets of ropes descended from it, three from either side. Almost as soon as they touched the ground, more people rappel down them. Weapons strapped to their back.

They were wearing matte black jumpsuits with body armour over the top and quickly surrounded me, weapons drawn. Expressionless helmets covered their heads and faces with black visors. Although they wore no obvious identification, I immediately know who they are. They are Gen-Corp security.

They quickly surround. 'Remain on the ground! Do not struggle,' a muffled female voice shouts and for a few terrifying seconds, I stare at a gun pointed squarely at my forehead. Are they going to kill me for running away? I worry about myself. Stupidly, I feel relief when another one produces a scanner and hustles up my sleeve, scanning the number tattooed on my forearm. She looks at the scanner and then talks into her radio.

'We have him, Ma'am. He is injured but alive.'

I have little time to worry about this when suddenly with a loud whizzing sound a rocket streaks across the sound and blows one engine off the side of the Gen-Corp hovercraft, with an almighty explosion and deafening whining sound the ship spins wildly as the pilots struggle desperately to regain control. They struggle in vain, however, and the ship careens through the sky before crashing with a massive explosion in a nearby field.

'Contact! Contact!' the soldier standing over me yells as a hail of bullets sends them scarpering for cover and dropping to the ground, desperate to get out of the open.

'Up you get,' the guard who found me demands.

'Can't,' I mutter squeezing my eyes shut as I try to block out the pain.

'Yes, you can,' hauling me up pain arks up my side with a groan I finally pass out.

The first thing I register is the smell of antiseptic. With a monumental effort I open my eyes.

'Oh, at last you are awake,' I turn to the voice and blink. Sat in a chair with a book in his lap is Aaron.

To be Continued

Milton Keynes UK
Ingram Content Group UK Ltd.
UKHW042137220823
427256UK00004B/207